I0625692

Mane Attraction

A Soulstealer Novella

NICOLETTE REED

Copyright © 2012 by Nicolette Reed
Edited by Sally Berneathy
Cover Art by Kim Killion of Hot Damn Designs

All rights reserved. This book or any portions thereof may
not be reproduced or used in any manner whatsoever
without the express written permission of the author except
for the use of brief quotations in critical articles or reviews.

This is a work of fiction. Names, places, businesses,
characters and incidents are either the product of the
author's imagination or are used in a fictitious manner. Any
resemblance to actual persons living or dead, actual events or
locales is purely coincidental.

EPub Edition November 2012 ISBN: 978-0-9856401-5-6
Print Edition ISBN: 978-0-9856401-6-3

PRAISE FOR FAE HUNTER

"Once you start reading Fae Hunter, you won't be able to put it down. The action starts on the first page and never lets up for the entire book. Just when you think you can take a deep breath and maybe even put the book down for the evening, a new twist erupts that makes you keep reading for one more chapter and one more chapter and one more chapter…"
-Romance and Mystery Author and Editor Sally Berneathy

"This book has so many surprises, twists, and turns, I couldn't put it down."
-Paranormal Romance Guild Reviews

"I think it's this love triangle that made the book for me."
-Fantasy and Romance Author J.F. Jenkins

"Great world-building, engaging characters that quickly draw you into the story, and enough twists and turns to keep you flipping the pages."
-Fantasy and Romance Author Crista McHugh

"…if you want a kick-ass heroine who struggles to do her best and save her world then you should definitely check this book – and series – out."
-The Flutterby Room Reviews

TITLES BY NICOLETTE REED

Fae Hunter (The Soulstealer Trilogy, Book #1)
Mane Attraction (A Soulstealer Novella, Book #1.5)

I hope that real love and truth are stronger in the end then any evil or misfortune in the world.
- Charles Dickens

CHAPTER ONE

The light grew brighter as Kit got closer and closer to the top of Lake Mavrovo. She didn't bother to look to see if her mother's guards had followed her. She swam as fast as she could, her chest thrust forward. She would see the sun again, even if only for a moment.

Kit crested the surface of the lake and cautiously looked around. Even though she was one of the most feared creatures in the Realms, she certainly didn't feel like it.

Gentle waves bobbed against the shoreline, beckoning her forth. It had been weeks since she set foot on firm ground, and she ached to feel the sand between her toes again. Entering the shallows Kit flung her long blue mane over her shoulder and focused on the ground solidifying beneath her. Gradually her lower half unknit to form two separate limbs. She stood, wobbly at first, and scooted further onto the sand before falling forward.

"How could I have forgotten how to walk already?" Kit ticked off on her fingers how long she thought she had been in the Realms. How many days had passed? It was hard to tell since she was always beneath the waters of Mavrovo, a place where the sun couldn't reach. She knew she looked older. Kit was eight years old when she had first entered the waters of Lake Mavrovo, and now she had developed to the point where she guessed she was about sixteen. Guess was all she could do. Time didn't work the same here.

The edge of the Riparian Forest stopped fifty feet away from Lake Mavrovo. Not even a leaf fell on its shores. There seemed to be a magical understanding that Lake Mavrovo was the territory of the selkie, the Riparian belonged to the elves, and never the twain shall meet.

When Kit came to the Realms it had all seemed a grand adventure. Now she was more isolated than in her former home, in the suburbs of Seattle. At least there she had friends. She didn't get to see her classmates that often because she had always been sick, but her friend Kieran had always made sure that no one took her seat.

"I saved a seat for you." Her eyes prickled with tears at the memory of her raven haired friend who never judged her like the others did. Finding out she was half-selkie and that her mother was the Queen of the selkies had been a tremendous shock, but it had explained her illnesses and made her feel less like a freak.

She wasn't ill anymore, but she sure was sick of being marooned without any sense of what her future would hold. At first her mother, Queen Elemi, had gone to considerable lengths to make sure she and her father fit in. A portion of the underwater castle had been transformed to look like her room at home. Her father Ralph, once a small town sheriff, had been given a position in the Queen's guard. The Queen could not take Ralph as her King because it was not allowed since he wasn't selkie, but she promised to keep him safe.

Ralph was happy. At least that was what he told Kit. She wasn't sure if he was happy or if he was doing what he needed to do to make sure Kit stayed alive. She would have died if she remained in Seattle. *Maybe that's what should have happened.* Kit tried to banish those thoughts from her mind, determined that her father's sacrifice would have meaning.

Every morning she awoke a little bit older, a little bit wiser. Elemi explained that, as a selkie, she would grow to maturity much faster than a human child. It was part of their defense mechanism. Selkies weren't very warm creatures. Children grew up fast and learned to take care of themselves. Kit had wanted a car for her sixteenth birthday. She got fins instead.

A branch cracked, returning Kit's attention to her surroundings. "Who's there?" She pulled at the sodden t-shirt she had on, trying to get it to cover her rear. The selkie swam around in nothing but their jewelry, but Kit still clung to her modesty and had insisted on the t-shirt. Her mother thought it silly but didn't keep her from it. At least when she was in the water, her lower half became fins and a tail like a mermaid. She had no qualms about that. Her shimmering scales covered her up. But out of the water she could form legs, apparently wobbly legs which were rather useless.

There was no answer from the brush. Probably only an animal. Kit spied what she had come for, a tree that seemed to defy the laws of magic and spread its branch across the divide just above the water's edge. The tree's fruit weighed the branch down so that Kit could almost touch it. She knew it was okay to eat. She had seen Valora, the fae who had brought her here, eat one before she left. The selkie diet was mostly meat and fish. Kit wanted to taste the flesh of the fruit more than anything, to feel its sweet juices running down the back of her throat.

She stood in the shallows, one foot in and one foot out of the water. Her mother had warned her that she was not to leave Mavrovo. She had put a charm, like a tracking device, on Kit to insure that she was always somehow within her grasp. At first being able to explore to the boundaries of Lake Mavrovo had scared Kit, now it suffocated her. After realizing that her kind rarely ventured above water, she felt she was drowning in it.

Her mother had told her that the charm was for her protection, but Kit was quickly finding out that the selkie were the ones others needed protecting from. Nope. Kit's mother wanted to keep tabs on her to make sure she wasn't an embarrassment or something. At least that was the only reason Kit could think of.

Kit stretched on her tiptoes and reached up. The smooth edges of the luscious red fruit teased the tips of her fingers but wouldn't allow her to grasp it.

▸◂

Damn! Mane had hoped the creature wouldn't hear the twig snapping. He crouched lower in the tall reeds on the bank of the lake. He didn't want her to know of his presence until he could figure out what kind of creature she was. Besides, he really enjoyed looking at her.

Mane swallowed a morsel of the fish he had collected that morning and watched the girl. She stood on her toes, trying to reach an asphodel fruit from the tree branch that hung above the water line. His gaze went to the shirt which clung to her chest and traced around one puckered nipple. The edge of the shirt rose up enough for him to see the curves of her bottom. *Stop thinking that way. She is barely more than a child and probably selkie.*

Mane finished the fish and wiped his hand down his bare chest. A streak of scarlet was left behind, proof that the levels of cinnabar in Mavrovo were on the rise. He'd come to Lake Mavrovo to collect his traps, hoping to get enough fish to feed his elven clan for a few days, though he'd have to toss out the ones with reddened flesh, the ones infected with cinnabar. The others wouldn't be able to stomach it.

Not his fault this delightful creature had come up just as he was getting ready to pull his traps from the water. Not his fault that her long blue hair hung down her back, and her wet t-shirt clung to her body, barely covering her rear. Not his fault he was forced to sit there and watch her delicious body.

He knew the cinnabar affected his better judgment, but it was also difficult to refuse a treat which he hadn't partaken of in so long.

She reached up and clutched the fruit as she stumbled forward onto the sand. A shockwave of light passed over the surface of the lake as her body left the water. In moments the selkie would be all over this beach. He had to make a decision quickly…leave or take a chance this creature could be of use to him.

He parted the reeds and dove into the lake, quickly crossing the short distance between himself and the girl. As Mane approached she grabbed something from the ground and threw it in his direction.

The overripe asphodel landed with a splat, its purple innards dripping down Mane's chest and immediately staining the fabric of his tan shorts which almost blended in with his skin color.

"How am I ever going to get that stain out?" Mane looked up at the girl.

"Oh, I'm so sorry. You scared me. I thought you were some monster." The girl's hands went from her face to her side and then up to her chest as if she couldn't decide whether to be scared, aloof, or demure. It was the combination of all three that made it clear she wasn't from around here.

"You don't have to worry about me. But you set off a selkie charm. There isn't much time before they come to see what it was. I recommend you hurry up and find your way home." Mane strode over slowly so he wouldn't startle the girl and reached his arm up to pick one of the asphodel fruits from a higher branch.

"And you should always pick the fruit from the higher branches. The ones this close to the lake have already gone rotten." Mane pointed to the muck on his chest.

"Did I make you bleed?" The girl put a hand out towards Mane's chest, but pulled it back as if he radiated heat. She stood with one foot crossed over the other, not necessarily the best position if you intended to make a run for it.

"No, that's my own mess. What exactly are you?" The girl's blue hair was unusual, as was the light in her blue-green eyes which looked up at him with wide-eyed curiosity.

"I'm selkie, or at least partly anyway. Are you an elf?" She reached up towards the point on the tip of Mane's ear, · and he instinctively pulled away.

"Yes, I am. Did you say you were selkie? I don't recall that your kind can be out of the water for long. And you generally don't have civil conversations with elves or wear t-shirts."

"I'm not exactly like the others. I didn't come from around here. My name is Kit. What's yours?" She gave him a smile and took a bite out of the asphodel. Her eyes closed briefly as she savored the sweet fruit.

"My name is Mane." He wanted to ask Kit where she had come from, but their conversation was over. Mane could see them moving through the water, getting closer. Any minute they'd surface. He moved away from the shoreline and further up onto the beach. If he touched the surface, the selkie would surely notice something was wrong with him, that he too wasn't from around here.

"Mane, they're going to make me go back, but I bet I can get away again. Do you want to meet here tomorrow? Same time? I'd love more of that fruit." She batted her eyelashes. The young thing was flirting with him. She was much too young, but she might be able to get him some information about the cinnabar. It wouldn't hurt to see.

"Yes, but bring me a fish from the lowest point you can find. You bring the fish." He reached up and picked another asphodel fruit, placing it gently into her outstretched hand. "I'll make sure you have plenty of fruit."

A flash went across the lake as the selkie started to rise. Their stark black eyes came just above the water line and Mane could tell that they were watching him, making sure he made no sudden moves against this girl. But he had no interest in her. He wanted to know about the cinnabar.

The girl nodded and as she dove into the water her legs knit together into a brilliant white fin. Iridescent scales glittered in the sunlight before disappearing into the water with a splash. The rest of the selkie melted back down into the water. It was too risky to retrieve his traps now, but hopefully after tomorrow, today's venture wouldn't end up being fruitless.

CHAPTER TWO

One of the larger guards took Kit by the wrist. She looked around for her father who held a high ranking position in the Guard. "Where is my father?" It never ceased to amaze Kit that she could talk and breathe underwater the same as she did above.

The selkie holding her dropped all his glamours. His large black eyes stared down and seemed to suck her in. His nose flattened and turned to slits. He smiled slightly, and Kit could see the sharp pointed teeth that were perfect for tearing flesh to bits in an instant. A shudder ran through her, but she didn't cry. She kept telling herself that it was better than being dead. Better than dead. Every day her mantra was tested.

The selkie said nothing and only continued to pull her down towards the bottom of Mavrovo. She didn't bother to fight. The entire Guard had been sent after her when her foot had left the water and set off the alarm. They were probably going to take her to her mother. She wouldn't get off easy, but it had been worth it. The elf. Mane. She chuckled to herself. Mane didn't even have any hair. His head was shaved bald. But she sure wasn't laughing at his body. Kit knew that men often walked around shirtless. It was just in the Pacific Northwest, where it tended to rain most of the year, there weren't too many opportunities to see ripped shirtless men walking around.

Of course, she had totally embarrassed herself by throwing rotten fruit at him. Kit smacked her free hand to her forehead. *He's going to think I am totally lame.* But she had gotten him to agree to meet her again tomorrow. She tried to keep that thought in the forefront of her mind as the castle came into view. Magical luminescence twinkled in sconces that were mounted around the perimeter of the castle. There was no natural light this far down underwater, but the selkie were not short on magic.

Kit searched amongst the Guards for her father. If he wasn't with them he normally stayed near the castle. Queen Elemi had imbued him with enough magic to allow him to live and breathe underwater like the rest of the selkie. Swimming around was a different problem. He was still a human. He could take a potion that would give him fins temporarily, but it didn't last long and he couldn't take it too often or it made him sick to his stomach.

The selkie's iron grip on Kit's wrist tightened as the group of them approached the castle gates which were always left open. The selkie had no natural enemies in Mavrovo. They were at the top of the food chain. Ralph, Kit's father, stumbled out of the front gates, catching himself on one of the bars.

"Kit, they found you. Good. We were all so worried."

He looked more than worried. His lips and chin trembled. Kit had a feeling she wasn't going to like whatever he had to tell her. "Darling, your mother wants to talk to you."

"Dad, do we have to?" Kit shrugged off the selkie who finally released his grip on her wrist. "Can't you tell Mom that I went up to get some asphodel fruit and I fell? It's the truth."

Ralph shook his head and looked down at his feet. "This day would have come regardless of what happened today, Kit. You need to talk to your mother."

He looked up at her and held out his hand. "I'll go with you. Don't be frightened."

Kit stopped being frightened a long time ago. She was accustomed to change at this point. Her father was still getting used to everything. She dismissed his behavior as nerves. It was probably good to get the talk with her mother over sooner rather than later. That way she would still have time to trap a fish for Mane. If she had knees they would have gone weak at remembering the small silver loop in his eyebrow. *His eyebrow is pierced. He is so cool.*

Kit followed her father into the castle, ignoring the twists and turns he made as he skipped past Queen Elemi's chambers and went deeper into the castle than Kit had ever been before. They stopped at a door and Kit looked around, trying to get her bearings.

"Where are we?"

"Your mother asked that I bring you directly down here." Ralph faced Kit, taking her arms in his hands. "You have to make the change, Kit."

The black eyes of the selkie that had dragged her down flashed through her mind. The fangs. The nose. "No, Dad, I won't become like them. I don't want to be a freak."

Her father pinched the bridge of his nose and tightly squeezed his eyes before erasing the lines from his face and replacing them with a too-quick smile. "Of course you would be concerned with how it would make you look. Kit, your mother can explain everything. She can answer all your questions. Nothing will be sprung on you when you go through that door, but you must go through it."

Kit gave a practiced nod. She knew it was no use going against her mother. Sneaking an asphodel fruit was one thing, this was another. She took a deep breath, out of habit, and they both entered the room.

Elemi was sitting on a throne which had been brought in for her while she waited for Kit. The shock of blue hair that Elemi had was so much like her own. There was no denying that this woman was her mother, and yet she had never felt a true connection to her. For whatever reason Elemi held Kit at a distance emotionally but still wanted her near physically.

"Looks as though the Guard has found you. Good thing. You almost missed your birthday."

"My birthday?" Kit tried to remember how long it had been since she had been brought to the Realms. It was confusing since no one cared about calendars here. Day and night blended together underwater, and she was always told where she was supposed to be. Not to mention that time seemed to plod along at a different pace here in the Realms. She had given up trying to keep track.

"Yes." Queen Elemi's smile was like that of a beauty queen acknowledging a crowd. It didn't reach her eyes. When her lips parted her fangs showed through, but Elemi still held her glamour in place for her daughter's benefit. Kit was grateful. The last thing she wanted was a glimpse at her future and who she might turn into. "It is the day I brought you into this world, and the day I gave you up to your father. Your sixteenth cycle is here. You must undergo the selkie sleep."

"What is that?"

The Queen rose from her throne and came closer to her.

Kit cast her eyes downward so she wouldn't be staring directly at her mother's naked chest. *Awkward.*

"Have you ever wondered why there are no children here?"

"I kind of figured you ate them," said Kit, realizing from the squint of her mother's eyes that her attempt at humor had failed.

Queen Elemi didn't skip a beat. "Children are weak and are targets for those who would wish us harm. Most children undergo the sleep after they are born, and it brings them to adulthood. After today's events I see now that I've been careless. I've allowed this to go on long enough. That elf you were talking to could have killed you right where you stood. My Guard confirmed that there would have been nothing they could have done to stop him. You need to undergo the change."

The blue-green of Elemi's eyes dimmed and faded into their true blackness. She was not giving Kit a choice. Ralph hadn't been totally honest. Her mother wasn't going to kill her. She just wanted to kill her childhood.

"So I have to go from being sixteen to what, exactly?" Kit had always looked younger than she was because her illness kept her thin. Her body had staved off puberty in order to try to keep her alive. She was sixteen, but she had the body of a twelve year old.

"I wish I could put you under long enough to bring you to full adulthood, but I have other matters to attend to. You will stay in the chamber overnight."

"But how old will I become?" Kit clutched at her mother's arm as she turned to leave the room.

"Selkies don't age as humans do, Kit. You are half human. I don't know how old you will be. The sleep will bring you closer to your selkie side. That is what is needed to keep you safe. I can't always send the Guard out after you. They will have more important matters to attend to soon enough. Your father will tuck you in." She nodded to Ralph who returned the gesture. He had clearly been given his orders.

Queen Elemi left the room in a hurry, a whoosh of bubbles following in her path. It was moments such as that which reminded Kit she lived underwater.

"Your mother promised you won't be hurt. You fall asleep and when you awaken you will be stronger and more powerful. There are a lot of vicious creatures out there, hon. I don't want you to get hurt."

"Dad, the selkie are some of the most vicious creatures in the Realms, and you want me to be more like them?" Kit knew the second the words left her mouth that she had touched a sensitive nerve in her father.

"I came here because I wanted you to be safe. I wanted you to live. You are selkie, Kit. It doesn't mean you have to be vicious. That part is up to you. You are still my daughter." Ralph stood up straighter and pushed his thumbs through his belt loops. Kit liked seeing him this way. It reminded her of his days as a sheriff. In Mavrovo he only got to play sheriff. There was no real need for him here. Actually, come to think of it, he was probably in more danger than she was.

If she added on a few more years maybe she could keep her father safe. Maybe the other selkie would stop looking at her and her father like they were easy targets. Like they were just waiting for Elemi to turn her back long enough to sneak a bite.

"I'll do it."

Ralph motioned to a small bed in the corner of the room. Next to the bed was a table with a vial of bright yellow liquid. "She said to drink that and you would fall asleep. I'll be here waiting for you when you wake up."

"Don't stay here all night or anything. You have to rest, too, Dad." Ralph only gave a small nod as Kit went to the table and picked up the vial. It was stoppered with a cork, and the liquid inside had a gelatinous quality.

"Bottoms up." Kit uncorked the vial and brought it to her lips. The yellow pudding slid into her mouth. "Ew, tastes like bananas." Bananas were the one thing Kit did not eat. Of course it had to taste like that. She tried to think of her father as she choked it down. She was doing this for him. She needed to protect him. The potion hit her like a ton of bricks. She sank down. Her limbs became leaden, feeling as though they were chained to the bed.

Ralph stood just outside of Kit's line of sight. She tried to move her head to see him, and the edges of her vision blurred. Darkness gradually descended.

Queen Elemi had said Kit was going into a selkie "sleep." Selkie sleep was anything but restful. It was the stuff of nightmares. The sounds of thunder shattered Kit's rest, but when she opened her eyes all she saw were streaks of purple and blue lightning in the sky above her head. Her limbs were still weighted down, and she couldn't move. The intensity of the thunder increased until the room vibrated with its power. The flashes of lightning struck closer.

Kit remembered a movie from when she was a child. One night she sneaked downstairs to watch television. Her father had already gone to bed. It was a horror movie about child ghosts who pulled people through the television, horrific clowns that hid under the bed, and a particularly frightening thunderstorm. The child in the movie was scared, and his mother told him that the timing between the lightning and the thunder indicated how close the storm was. So Kit couldn't help but watch the lightning streak across the sky and count the seconds before the thunder clapped. Her eyelids clamped down tight, like the hatch door on a storm shelter.

In the movie, it didn't end well. A tree broke through the window and started to devour the child. Kit took a deep breath, filling her lungs to bursting. There were no trees here. Only blackness and thunder and lightning which were devouring her youth. Another clap of thunder shook her to the very core. Her body was still quivering when she opened her eyes again and saw the lightning come down directly on top of her.

The jagged bolts squeezed down tight like a boa constrictor preparing to consume its next meal. Kit clenched her jaw and waited for the pain, but all she felt was pressure. The surface of her skin was cold, but deep inside a storm was aching to release itself, and only Kit's will kept it at bay. The lightning glowed and pulsated, and at some point she passed out altogether.

When Kit opened her eyes she saw that she was still in the same room. An empty vial sat on the bedside table. Kit sat up and a weight at her chest made her shoulders roll forward.

"Holy crap, I have boobs." She grabbed them as if they weren't actually attached to her and might pop off like some silly novelty item. Nope, they were attached. Firmly. Her t-shirt, which had once skirted her bottom, now barely skirted her midriff. Kit grabbed at her face, feeling for some sign of age. Maybe wrinkles or sagging skin. She touched her nose. At least that was still there and seemed unchanged. She looked around for a mirror and suddenly realized that there was something else that was missing. Someone terribly important. Her father.

෨ஃ

"If you bring nothing back tonight, it will be a week without food. You know what that means for your mother and your sister. I am too old to go on the hunt. If you need help then talk to Pawel or Torkel. They both have offered to go along with you." Mane's father reached out from beneath the covers and patted Mane's hand. He looked so much older than the last time Mane saw him. The elves were suffering. Food was scarce, and it was only getting worse.

The animals of the forest had fled. Soil could no longer support the crops. The only source of food seemed to be the birds in the trees, and they were starting to figure that out. Not even the elves, who lived long lives, could live very long without food.

"If I take Pawel and Torkel they will only steal whatever I hunt to feed their own families. They only want to come with me to learn how it is I have been feeding you what little I can find. They don't wish to help us, Father." Mane patted his father's hand and saw that the bluish veins he had noticed pulsing beneath the skin had become brighter. His skin was thinner.

"Yes, well, if our situation doesn't change soon we will have to leave this place."

"And go where? The Dragonlands? Mount Elbrus? The Riparian is our home, Father. It's been home to the elves for centuries. I will find out what is causing this."

Mane's father nodded and rolled onto his side, falling asleep once more. It seemed that all he did was sleep lately. Mane couldn't help but feel guilty. He knew he didn't bring this plague onto the elves. He knew he shouldn't even care, but he had spent the better part of the last fifty cycles with these people, and they were the closest he was ever going to get to home again.

The cinnabar infected the land and was chasing away the animals. He wasn't sure what was happening in Mavrovo that was causing the red dust to rise. Hopefully the girl would bring him the fish, and he could convince her to invite him down under her protection. He knew that to go down into the selkie territory without being asked would be suicidal.

Mane rose from his father's bed and paused as he reached the doorway to the small hut his father had sequestered himself to ever since he fell ill. He watched the slow rise and fall of his father's form under the thin sheet. He owed his continued existence to this man.

He let the curtain fall across the doorway and set out towards the edge of the Riparian. The only way he was ever going to find an answer to what was poisoning the land would be by gaining access to Mavrovo, and the strange girl, Kit, was the only selkie he had ever met who spoke to him.

Mane made his way to the shore where he'd met Kit the day before. It was quick work to collect a basket of asphodels which left him with time to spare. After checking the traps and collecting another fish laden with cinnabar, he climbed into a tree so he could survey the shore while keeping himself hidden. After a few hours the branch pressing into his shoulders started to become painful. Splashes of orange and purple appeared as the sun set on the horizon. There still wasn't any sign of Kit.

He swallowed the last of the fish and poked through the basket of asphodels he had collected for her. Unfortunately, they weren't palatable for the elves. They were mostly suitable for feeding the animals that the elves hunted, but these were desperate times. He might have to resort to convincing his mother and sister to eat them so they wouldn't starve since the cinnabar laced fish was off limits to them.

"Is that your trick? Hanging out in the trees all day and acting like a bird?"

"Maybe you would have better luck if you rolled yourself in mud and tacked on some feathers. They're not going to think a bald elf like you is any kind of bird."

Heat flushed through Mane's body and he tried to ignore the twitch in his fist. He knew Pawel and Torkel had followed him before, but he certainly didn't want their interruption tonight especially since he was still hoping Kit would show up. He leapt down from the tree and landed in front of them without a sound. Pawel and Torkel were his playmates growing up. They were twins, and both kept their black hair long as most of the elven men did. Mane had shorn his hair as soon as he was declared an adult. He knew he wasn't like the others, and they had always treated him as different even though they didn't know the truth, so why make any sort of effort to blend in?

"What are you two doing here?" Mane stood and looked down on them. He was a foot higher than the both of them and brought himself up to his full height.

"Hunting. There is no reason we can't be here hunting the same as you. That is what you are doing, isn't it?" Pawel took a step towards Mane and stared right back at him.

"Looks as though he is hunting asphodel fruits." Torkel held the basket of asphodel in one hand while he tossed one of the fruits up and down with the other. "Oops." He let the basket tip, the fruits spilling to the ground. He took a step and squished one of them beneath his boot.

The brothers always seemed to relish antagonizing Mane. He usually did his best to ignore them, but they had gone too far. Food was scarce and they were wasting it just because they wanted to oust him from his place in the clan. They knew once his father died he would be named the clan leader. If Mane was gone they would be the ones sharing that position. Mane would gladly let them have it if he didn't think they would make things worse for the clan than they already were.

Mane rushed towards Torkel and grabbed him by the shirt, lifting him in the air before he could reach for his bow. He scratched at Mane's bare chest, trying to find purchase on something to stop Mane from choking him to death. Pawel jumped on Mane's back and pulled at Mane's arms, trying to get him to release his brother.

"Let go of him, Mane. You aren't doing your father any favors."

Before Mane could process Pawel's request, he heard him scream out as he was ripped from Mane's back. Torkel's eyes went wide, and he passed out in Mane's arms. Mane shoved him forward and hid the both of them behind the tree trunk as he peered out to see who their attacker was.

He saw no one. The light in the sky had dimmed. On the ground where he had been standing was a small puddle of dark liquid. It only took Mane a few inhales to realize it was blood. Fresh blood. Likely Pawel's blood. Mane only had a small knife on him. He reached down and took the bow and sling of arrows from around Torkel's shoulder.

The dried wood of the cheap bow creaked as Mane pulled the string taut. He only hoped he wouldn't crack the damn thing in half before he could get a shot off. There was a reason he didn't usually use these things. He broke more of them than he cared to admit.

A figure dashed from the brush and headed for the water line. Mane let the arrow loose and the bow cracked, sending his arrow off target. Instead of hitting the creature in the heart it shot through its shoulder, but it was enough to bring it down.

Mane pulled his knife from the sheath at his thigh and ran towards the creature to finish the job. With any luck the beast would have enough meat to make it worth all the trouble, but he needed to finish it off first.

As he approached he saw the creature was lying on its stomach. It was crawling towards the water at a wounded pace. He grabbed the arrow and used it to flip the beast over so he would have a clear shot at its heart. In the dark it was impossible to tell what it was, but he knew it had attacked them and that it was large enough to feed more than just his family.

"Mane, no!"

Mane froze, the knife in his hand mere inches from the creature's chest. "Who are you?"

"It's Kit."

CHAPTER THREE

The light from the moon was starting to appear through the trees. Kit could clearly see the sculpted muscles of Mane's chest even though he hadn't yet focused on her. She put her hand down the front of her shirt and pulled out the wilmot she had managed to catch as she left the castle. "I brought you the fish."

Mane looked towards the left and saw the legs of Pawel sticking out from the brush. "What did you do?"

Kit sat up and brushed the back of her wrist across her mouth. It came away slick with blood. "He was hurting you. I don't know."

Her voice trembled as she held the wilmot and stared at her bloodied hand. The arrow was still stuck in her shoulder, but she could barely feel it.

Simultaneous waves of anger, doubt, frustration, and fear had washed over her when she saw Mane being attacked from behind. The same feelings which had driven her away from the castle even though she had not yet found her father. It was like the worst PMS ever, and she desperately wanted to be far away from Mavrovo. She didn't want to be a danger to him.

Kit touched the sharpened points of her canine teeth which she had sunk into the elf's neck without a thought. The memory of his blood gushing forth into her mouth gave her an erotic shudder. In seconds he had been a limp rag in her hands.

"Stay here and stay quiet." Mane slipped his knife into the sheath at his thigh before slinging Pawel's limp body over his shoulder.

Kit slapped her hand over her mouth to cover her fangs and to hold in the scream which threatened to erupt. She had killed another, but that fact wasn't what bothered her the most, it was her reaction to that killing.

The blood dripped from her wrist and spattered the white scales adorning her lap where a different kind of heat was building. She tried to brush it away along with the sensations that had welled up between her thighs. She ripped the arrow from her shoulder, causing a ripple of pain that seemed to bring her back into focus.

Kit crept forward and peered through the underbrush at Mane who was talking to the other elf.

"There are many hungry things out in the woods besides us elves. I wasn't able to catch it, but you should take Pawel's body to camp. I will remain and hunt down the beast that did this."

Torkel stood his ground. "If you think I am going to let you hunt the beast that killed my brother, you are mistaken. You can deliver his body and tell my father I won't be rejoining him until I have this beast's head with me. I saw it, you didn't. It was a selkie, and it's above water. It won't last long, and I can guard the water line until it tries to return. Give me my arrows."

Torkel put his hand out. Mane looked at his feet, and

muttered something incomprehensible like he was looking for the right words to say. He was trying to protect her. He could easily have told the elf that she was the one responsible. Let him hunt her down.

In an instant Kit was by his side. "You don't want to hunt down the creature. It is too dangerous. It is better that one of you should live to fight and feed your family than both of you should die. Let Mane take that chance if he is willing. Your brother deserves a proper burial."

Torkel's gaze became fixed and dazed, and he repeated each sentence as Kit recited it. He dropped his hand to his side, picked up his brother's body and walked into the Riparian.

"Don't ask me how I did that." Kit sat on the ground and shoved her hands under her chin. She looked down and realized that her selkie tail had become legs, except scales still covered the area between her waist and her upper thighs. So basically she was wearing a tube top and a mini skirt, stained with blood. Looking like a hooker on her first date shouldn't have concerned her as much as killing the elf, but it did. She felt nothing. No remorse. She had truly become a monster.

Mane knelt down beside Kit, finally taking the wilmot from her hand. "You look nothing like you did yesterday. Exactly what happened to you?"

He reached forward and brushed a lock of her blue hair behind her ear as he tipped her chin up to meet his gaze.

"No, I shouldn't look at you." Kit stared down into her lap.

"Your charms won't work on me, Kit. I'm a bit different than the other elves."

Kit studied Mane's face. He was as gorgeous as he was when she saw him yesterday. Light glinted off the small ring pierced through his left eyebrow. His shoulders were broad.

She followed the lines of his abs down to his narrow waist. Despite what had just happened he seemed calm. Self-contained. A skill Kit seemed to be greatly lacking considering what had just happened. A skill she needed if she was going to be able to help her father.

"You do look different than those other two."

"Yes, thank goodness." He rubbed his hand over his bald head. "You need to return to Mavrovo, Kit. It isn't safe for you here. Your power of suggestion won't work for long after the elders have a chance to talk to Torkel."

"But I can't. I don't know what's happening to me." Kit's breath burst in and out of her chest as if she were on the verge of tears.

"You do realize you have breasts now, right?" The timbre of Mane's voice dropped lower in time with his gaze over her body. He cleared his throat, but there was no erasing his obvious intent.

Kit quickly folded her arms over her chest, but wasn't able to do a very good job of hiding herself. Mane's leer seemed to catch them both off guard. She felt her face flush. Her senses sharpened and she heard Mane swallow.

"These I get." Kit grabbed at her chest for emphasis. "The killing and drinking blood, I am a little fuzzy on. Oh, and the fact that killing that elf..." Kit crawled over to Mane and closed the distance between them. "...was the hottest thing ever." She placed a finger on Mane's lips, drew it slowly down his neck and trailed it over his chest.

"See, what the heck is wrong with me?" Kit sat back and crossed her hands over her chest again.

"Have you never seen other selkies do this?" Mane asked. He adjusted his shorts before gesturing towards the lake.

Kit shook her head. "No, they eat meat of creatures we

catch in the lake, but they don't do what I just did. At least not that I have seen."

"I suppose it would be more common with prey out of water. Selkies are not often out of water."

"Not all selkie happen to have an amulet from the Queen that allows them to do so. Plus, I always thought maybe I could be out of water longer because of, well, I'm special, too." Kit knew better than to share all of her secrets with this elf. She had only met him yesterday. Her mother had been abundantly clear that any abomination, that is, any half-human creature, found in the Realms was put to death.

"It's okay. We both have our secrets." Mane stood up. "I am sure your mother will explain it all to you and tell you that you are normal. Thank you for the fish. I had a basket of asphodel for you, but those two ruined them."

"Then you still owe me." Kit jumped up and blocked Mane's path. He looked down at her, a smirk forming in the corner of his mouth.

"What is it you want in return?" Mane raised the fish.

"My mother will tell me this is all normal, to kill a creature and enjoy it. She did this to encourage the vicious side of me, I know it. I want you to teach me self-control. You seemed to have a lot of it when dealing with those two jerks." Kit held her breath as she waited for his response.

Mane gave a sigh. "I suppose we can meet again tomorrow, but the others will know to look for me here. Another place?"

"Can you get to the portal at the center of the Riparian?"

"Yes."

"Then I'll meet you there." Kit stood up and placed a quick kiss on Mane's lips before letting out a giggle and running towards the water's edge. As she entered she turned and raised her arm above her head to wave to Mane, knowing full well that the bottom edge of her breasts would be visible as she did so. Kit might need Mane to help her learn self-control, but she was already learning the benefits of being a woman.

❧

Mane watched as Kit waved to him and couldn't help but notice all her new curves, but she was still so young. Yesterday she had been a child. Mane shook his head. How would he explain Pawel's death? This wasn't going to bode well for relations between the selkie and the elves. It wasn't that the elves had ever been allies of the selkie, but they both left each other alone. The only ones the elves quarreled with were the orcs and trolls that acted like bored children and often killed things for the simple joy of it.

He set the fish down on a flat rock and pulled the knife from the sheath at his thigh. He pressed the tip of the sharpened blade into the fish's gut and drew it down slowly. The skin fell away all too easily and inside was exactly what Mane had feared.

The fish was completely gorged with cinnabar. The red mineral was not only in the fish's belly, but also within its gills and woven into its flesh. The cinnabar had to have been flowing strong for a while in order to cause this much infection. It confirmed his suspicions about why the animals had fled the Riparian, why the crops wouldn't grow, and why he was no longer able to see through the veil between worlds. The gods down under in Acheron were growing in strength.

"What are you doing here, demon?"

Mane's head shot up to follow the sound of the voice which seemed to come from no particular direction. He gripped the knife in his hand which was still covered in a thick coating of the liquid cinnabar, a blood red mix which was deadly to most creatures except for those that lived within Mavrovo and under it. And those like him.

"I'm up here, demon."

Mane looked up and saw the outstretched white wings of a fae hovering above him.

"I should be asking you the same thing, priest. Since when do the fae grace Underworld with their presence? I don't remember when I last saw one of your kind."

The fae landed on the ground a comfortable distance from where Mane stood. The fae seemed harmless, but Mane still clutched the knife in his hand.

"I have come to deliver a message, but I can see right through you, demon."

"This form was not my choosing. It was punishment because I don't see eye to eye with the others." Mane could feel his eyes flare red. He had indulged in far too much cinnabar lately, and it was bringing out the demon inside him, a fact he hid remarkably well since he was reborn in the body of the elf he inhabited.

"Maybe so. What are your intentions with the selkie girl?"

"Kit? She wanted to know how to control her demons. I seemed to be the best suited to help her with that." Mane's jaw stiffened. He didn't like having to explain himself to this fae, but he didn't want to quarrel with a magic user. This fae had magic deep within his bones which echoed off of him in waves that made Mane dizzy.

The fae's golden eyes sparkled as he tipped his head from side to side and appraised Mane. "My name is Pryn. I am the high priest of Dell'Aria. I have brought this invitation to Kit for the wedding of the princess Valora. It will be taking place within the fortnight. Do you think she will be ready to attend the ceremony? Be amongst people?"

Mane laughed as he took the paper from the priest. "So I have to get Kit ready for a wedding? Funny, I was thinking more along the lines of preparing her to live out the rest of her life with a vicious beast inside her. But I suppose it can be done. I've just met the girl, I know nothing of her resolve."

"I'll let Kit tell her own tales, but suffice it to say she is very brave. Understand this, I can accept your intentions towards the selkie girl, but where Valora is concerned you will stay far away."

"How would I ever get the chance to meet her anyway?"

"It seems demons have a way of wiggling into her life." Pryn bolted upwards and disappeared into the sky overhead. The fae had always been unusual in their ways and made Mane uncomfortable. They worshiped the Goddess Varuna and even though Mane had been branded a traitor because he did not agree with the Demon King Ravanna, it didn't mean he was on Varuna's side either.

Angels and demons were very real. You just couldn't be too certain which was good and which was evil.

Mane shoved a wad of the wilmot fish into his mouth and put the paper into his pocket. Returning to camp was not an option at this point. He had ingested too much of the cinnabar, and the demon flare would scare the other elves. Best to stay away tonight and keep up the charade that he was hunting down the beast that killed Pawel.

He certainly did want to hunt Kit down. Hunt her down and pin her to the ground. Mane adjusted his pants again and tried to push the thoughts of Kit out of his mind. He was going to be her teacher. She was going to be his student. That was all. And he would get her to bring him to Mavrovo so he could see the extent of what Ravanna had done.

Mane entered the Riparian and started on his trek to the center.

CHAPTER FOUR

Kit returned to Mavrovo, but everything had changed. The world through a teenager's eyes was very different from the world through that of a woman. Kit knew her mother would want to see her so her first task was to find and appease the Queen. Her next task would be to get her to allow Kit to use the portal that opened up in the center of the Riparian. That would be much more difficult.

As she got closer to the castle, Kit noticed the selkies all turning to observe her. One by one she looked into their eyes which all held an identical reddish glow, similar to the glowing red dust which ebbed through cracks in the sediment that surrounded the castle. It was as if she was descending into hell. She wasn't sure how long she would be able to take being down here.

The hall outside her mother's room was empty, which was unusual. She peeked into the room and saw Queen Elemi staring down into a swirling vortex of red energy in the middle of her room.

"Is that all you're going to tell me? How will I know what I am supposed to do next?" shouted Elemi.

A deep, booming voice came blasting out of the vortex, pushing Elemi onto the floor. "The time has not yet come. You will know when it does."

In an instant the floor returned to normal. Kit stood up and counted to ten before knocking on her mother's door. "Mom, are you in there?" She gently pushed the door open and saw that Elemi had set herself at her vanity and was pulling a brush through her long blue locks.

Elemi's expression in the mirror went from anger to joy. "My dear Kit, look at you! You have become a full-grown selkie. There is no denying you are my progeny." She rose from the stool in front of the mirror and gestured to the chair. "Come and sit, there is much we must talk about."

Kit gingerly crossed the floor where the swirling vortex once was. She was pretty certain that what she had just seen would not be one of the topics of their conversation.

Kit sat down at the vanity and got a close look at herself in the mirror for the first time since the change. Her eyes and her hair were the same, but her cheekbones seemed more defined. She slid her right hand down the side of her face and across her lips which seemed to hold a deeper red tint than they had before.

"You have fed already. I expected that the hunger would strike you, but I thought I would be able to show you first." She ran the brush through Kit's hair.

"I'm sure a Queen has a lot of important responsibilities." Kit tried to dampen the disrespectful tone from her voice. The last thing she needed was to anger her mother.

"Nothing as important as preparing you for your life as a selkie. You are one of us now."

"Where are all the guards?"

The brush stopped mid-stroke. Kit froze hoping she

hadn't asked the wrong question. "We have had to send out more selkies through the portals to find food. We need to be strong for challenges that await us. The usual fare isn't going to be enough." Elemi stared at Kit in the mirror.

"Is my father with them?"

"No. Your father has been put in stasis, Kit. He is safe."

"Can I see him?" Kit's voice came out just above a whisper.

Elemi set the brush on the vanity. "It would not be a good idea. Focus on your new role. You have fed on the blood of another creature of the Realms, have you not?"

Kit noticed her lips were the color of blood, a stark contrast to her pale white skin. When she was ill as a child she had also been pale. But she felt anything but ill now, and she was no longer young. She felt strong with the knowledge of a decade of years thrust upon her all at once and the blood of the fae coursing through her veins. "Yes, but I didn't mean to kill him."

"That is your only mistake, Kit. You were meant to kill him. You did as the selkies have done for centuries. You lure your prey in with your powers of persuasion and then you drain them of their life. It is the only way we can survive. We can live on other forms of nourishment for a short while, but the only way we can truly be what we are meant to be is to drain the life force of another."

"I have to kill others so I can live." It was more of a statement than a question. Kit knew it to be true. The few months she had been in Mavrovo since she had been brought here from Earth were an eye-opening experience, to say the least. Now she was being told what she feared the most, that she was just like them. Underwater vampires.

"Yes, but you have an ability most selkies do not. Because you are half-human you are able to be away from

Mavrovo longer than most. My amulet will extend your reach even farther. It is very important that you help the selkies, Kit."

"Does this have anything to do with all that red stuff that is coming through the cracks outside the castle? What's happening to our home?"

Elemi cracked a small smile. "Don't worry about that, Kit. The cinnabar will only serve to strengthen us. Our home will always be here, but what if we could call more of this world our home? Wouldn't it be nice not to have to be tethered to these waters?"

Elemi didn't wait for Kit to respond. "I'm going to check on the guards and see how they are faring. Mother is hungry."

"But wait, Mom, I was hoping that I could...um...go hunting again. I'm pretty hungry, too. Maybe since I can walk around I could hunt in the Riparian? I had an elf earlier, and he was delicious." Kit tried to make her plea sound convincing. Remorse was not coming easily, but she certainly didn't relish the idea of killing.

Elemi paused. "Bring one for me. I haven't had an elf in ages. So difficult to catch. Well done, my darling." She pulled a small chest from the shelf. Inside were several vials of greenish-gold liquid. "Give whatever elf you bring with you this potion. It will allow him to breathe the waters of Mavrovo long enough so that I can properly sink my teeth into him."

"Yes, Mother." Kit watched as her mother left. There was only one elf she intended to seek out, and she certainly wasn't going to bring him down to meet her mother. However, she slipped the vial into the scales around her waist and watched as they magically closed around it.

"So cool not to need pockets anymore." Kit picked up

the brush and continued to stroke her hair. She wanted to help her father, but the best way to help him would be to learn some self-control first. If she didn't she might turn on her father, and she knew she would never forgive herself if she did that. Though learning self-control around Mane might prove to be difficult.

∂∞∽

Mane plunged another sharpened stick into the ground. His hands were becoming raw with the constant whittling he had been doing for the last several hours. It took the entire night to travel to the middle of the Riparian to the portal at the center. The Riparian was a large forest and home to many creatures other than the elves, some who would rather kill first and talk later.

After arriving unscathed at the portal entrance, he set his back to a nearby rock and continued to carve the sticks he had collected into sharpened stakes. He had no intention of using them, but he wasn't stupid. Kit was now a selkie, much different and far less innocent since the first time he had met her. To succeed at teaching her control he would have to test her limits. Mane was going to try hard not to enjoy the task.

He slung the knife into the ground and reached his hands again towards the portal. He wasn't able to activate them, but he could sense where they were and when they were active. Nothing. He reached into his satchel and pulled out a warm asphodel fruit. "Maybe this will get my mind off things." Mane knew he had eaten too much of the wilmot, and the cinnabar coursing through his veins would do nothing to assist in keeping his demonic whims at bay. He had many cycles to learn self-control. Now this little selkie might just be the one to break him, and he didn't mind the thought.

He clamped his mouth down on the lukewarm flesh of the asphodel fruit and immediately gagged. It was sickly sweet. His palate had already become accustomed to the cinnabar laced flesh of the fish he had been poaching from Mavrovo.

"Damn you, Ravanna." He was spitting out the last of the fruit when the portal sprang to life. Mane snatched his knife from the ground and hid it away at the sheath on his thigh, pulling his shorts over the top to keep it covered.

A slender, pale foot snaked out of the portal and tested for solid ground followed by the rest of Kit who was dressed the same as she had been the day before. Mane tried to keep his pulse at a steady pace. As a selkie she would be able to sense the slightest change in his physical response. He needed to keep the upper hand if he was going to convince her to take him down to Mavrovo.

"Hi, Mane!" She bounded over and wrapped her arms around his neck, giving him a big hug and pressing her firm breasts into his chest, only a small layer of cotton between him and her perky nipples.

He grasped her shoulders and slowly pushed away her embrace. "First of all, keep your distance from people. The closer you are, the easier it will be for you to lose control." A fact Mane had learned the hard way many times over and one of the reasons why it had been so long since he had been this close to a woman.

"Right, sorry." Kit put her hands to her side and looked up into Mane's eyes. He was glad that her gaze held no influence over him. Her body was doing enough in that area. "So where do we start?"

"Our lessons will be rushed. Apparently I'm supposed to be getting you ready for this." Mane handed Kit the slip of paper that Pryn had given to him announcing the wedding of

35

Valora and Dooley.

She jumped up and down as she read it. "Are you serious? Where the heck did you get this? This is so awesome."

"A fae priest gave it to me and asked that I be of assistance in preparing you to control yourself so that you can attend."

Kit's head dropped. She worried at the edges of the paper. "I am really concerned about that myself." She looked up into Mane's eyes with a cold steely set in her gaze. "I didn't feel bad about killing that elf. It was like biting into a hamburger. I should have felt remorse, but I didn't. I wonder if the selkie sleep has taken the last of my humanity." She gasped and brought her hand to her mouth.

"Humanity?" Mane cocked his head to the side and studied her further. Without her confession he would never have known, thinking her only to be a young selkie. But now he knew why he was so affected by the little selkie. Humans were the reason Mane had disagreed with Ravanna and had been banished into the body of this elf. One human in particular.

"I didn't mean to tell you." She brought her hand down from her mouth. "But I think I can trust you."

Trust, another unique and human quality. "Yes, you can trust me, Kit. I mean you no harm. I find humans fascinating, and I guarantee you that you have not lost all your humanity. We just have to wake it up a little bit."

"Is there a way that I can survive without having to kill anybody?"

It was a question he had hoped would come later, but Kit was as anxious to learn as he was to get to Mavrovo. "You will always require the blood of another to sustain you. But humans eat animals, do they not?"

Kit nodded. "So I could eat meat and that would be okay?"

"No, you need blood, Kit. Blood." Mane let the word hang in the air for a moment as he tried to keep the blood from rushing to his nether regions. The thrill of killing had always been a part of him, and he had done a good job at keeping himself under control. Teaching another would help renew those lessons. Kit needed to learn control and Mane needed a strong reminder. "But you can control who and what you hunt and control the cravings so that you won't hurt anyone unnecessarily. There are many ways to keep the demon inside you from waking, so to speak."

"Are those one of the ways?" Kit pointed to the sharpened stakes that Mane had arranged in a circle on the ground.

"Those are your first lesson. Step inside the circle." Kit hopped over the small barrier of foot long spikes and stood in the middle. The circle was about half the size of the small clearing they were in. Enough room for Kit to take several steps in each direction from the center.

"When did you last feed?"

"From the elf last night."

"Good. Stay here. When I return you must force yourself to stay inside the circle. There will be a strong temptation to leave it, but know that there will be repercussions if you do."

"You going to punish me if I step outside?" Kit dangled her foot over the boundary line.

A growl pulsed forth from Mane's throat as he bolted to the edge of the circle and got within an inch of Kit's face. "This will never work if you don't take it seriously. And yes, I mean to punish you, and you won't like it."

"You don't know me very well." Kit placed her foot on

the ground and took two steps back, clutching her hands together in front of her and pressing her breasts together as she cocked her head to the side.

"I'll return shortly." Mane stalked into the forest and tried to ignore the raw ache coursing through him. He returned to his intended prey, a small buckrabbit that had been hiding in a nearby hollow log ever since Mane had entered the clearing. It was likely hoping Mane would pass by and it could escape unnoticed, but this buckrabbit was Kit's first test.

છ∼ગ

Kit cursed under her breath as Mane disappeared into the tree line. *Way to go, bonehead, you totally scared him off.* Of course he would have no reason to like her. She had killed one of his people, and now he was in trouble because of her. In fact, it seemed strange that he would want to help her at all. What did he have to gain from it?

Kit fidgeted with the amulet at her neck. Her mother would expect her to have an elf with her when she returned, but she would have to make an excuse. Maybe tell her that she couldn't catch anything and hope her mother couldn't tell she was lying.

Before Kit had too much time to think about any of it Mane stepped through the trees holding a large rabbit in his hands. The creature's feet pawed at the air as it struggled to free itself.

"I can't eat that rabbit," said Kit.

Mane chuckled. "And why not?"

"Because it is a bunny. Are you kidding? It's way too cute to eat. And it's so scared."

"So you feel badly for it?"

Kit paused. "I guess I do. So why can I feel bad for a

bunny but not for an elf?"

"I think if you were hungrier you probably wouldn't feel so sorry for it." Mane reached down and pulled the knife from the sheath at his thigh. Kit's gaze followed the muscles in his biceps as he clutched the knife in one hand and the long ears of the rabbit in the other.

She suddenly realized what he intended to do and took a step outside the circle. "No, don't."

Mane held up the knife, tightly clenched in his fist. "Control yourself, Kit."

Kit hesitated and brought her foot inside the circle. "You don't have to kill it." Her voice was barely above a whisper. Tears dripped down her cheek.

"You are a selkie, Kit. It is in your nature to kill. Remember this moment. Remember the fear that the creature feels. You can hear its heart beating fast. It knows that each breath it takes might be its last. Close your eyes and keep them closed."

Kit did as Mane instructed and squeezed her eyes tighter as she heard a small squeak and then nothing. For a few moments, there was only silence. Then she heard the dried leaves crunch under Mane's feet as he approached her.

The scent of iron tickled at the edge of her reach. She inhaled deeply, and it was suddenly all around her, making her blood run hot. Her few items of clothing were suffocating, and she wanted to crawl right out of her skin.

"Open your eyes and stay still." That was the last thing Mane said before Kit flung herself at him and tossed him on his back. Her fangs extended. She clawed and scratched at him for the rabbit whose blood poured forth from the slice Mane had made in its neck.

Mane tossed Kit off him with an unnatural strength, and she landed inside the circle for an instant. Then Mane was down upon her, pressing her back against the tree trunk and holding her wrists above her head with one hand. He pulled a sharpened stake from the ground and she let her fingers close down around it as he placed it into her hand. He eased his hold on her wrists, but still kept her body in place with a strong hand gripping her waist.

"Press the stake into your hand. Focus on your own pain. Focus on your own blood. Its scent will help you control your hunger."

Kit didn't want to control her hunger. She wanted to suck the rabbit dry. Mane clutched Kit's face in his hand and forced her to turn and look at him. "You do want to control yourself, right?"

Kit saw that blood had splattered onto Mane's chest. His muscles strained from holding her down. She had no idea the kind of strength she possessed. It must be a lot if she could cause Mane to tremble slightly. She could sense he was weakening his grip. If only she could get some of the blood she could control herself. That was what she needed, not to stab herself with a sharp stick.

She continued to struggle against his grip and then thought better, dropping her head to his chest. The warmth of blood mingled with the salty sheen of sweat that had formed across the top of Mane's pecs drew her demon to the surface. Her tongue flicked out over her sharpened fangs and slowly licked the droplets from his skin.

A low growl pulsed through Mane's throat, causing her to stop for a moment before continuing. The wind was knocked out of Kit's lungs as he tossed her onto her back and pressed his full body weight on her.

"If you won't do it, I will." He pulled another stick from the ground, plunging it into Kit's hand.

The lust for blood was replaced in an instant with a

searing pain. Kit suddenly realized what she had been doing a second earlier. It was as if a fog had been lifted. She could still smell the rabbit, but she could also interpret it as what it was. Before she had been under a spell that pulled her in only one direction. Now she saw the options in front of her. The choice. That, and the stake in her hand hurt like hell.

"Exactly how long do I have to be impaled?" Kit didn't mention that Mane was still lying on top of her because she didn't really mind that. Wouldn't mind if he impaled her with something else.

"It is one way of controlling yourself around the blood. If you remove the distraction, you will fall into the bloodlust again unless you satiate that craving."

&oᴕ

Mane had hoped she would do better. It was probably because of the cinnabar that she lacked so much self-control. The rabbit was nothing compared to what she would encounter in the real world. There wasn't going to be much hope for her being able to attend the wedding at this rate.

"You said there was another way to control the bloodlust. What is that?" Kit wiggled her body underneath Mane, and he realized he was probably squeezing the breath out of her. He reached over and grabbed the rabbit, handing it to her.

"It's not appropriate."

Kit pulled the stake from her hand and reached for the rabbit. She locked her gaze on Mane as she sank her teeth into the neck of the tiny creature and pulled the last drop of blood from its body. She brought her mouth away from its neck. Her lips were stained with bright red blood.

"So you won't tell me what my other options are? I thought you were supposed to be my teacher." She flung the body of the rabbit to the side and pulled herself up into a seated position, crossing her arms across her chest and pushing her bottom lip out in a sullen pout.

The sight of the blood mixed with the cinnabar coursing through Mane's veins was almost too much. Mane pulled himself onto all fours and crawled towards Kit. "It wouldn't be right. You are so young."

Kit watched Mane slink towards her, and a light bulb seemed to go on in her head. "You don't know how much I want you to teach me." Kit grabbed the edges of her shirt and pulled it over her head, tossing the crumpled fabric to Mane who caught it and squeezed it into a ball as he tried to decide what he should do.

She reclined on a boulder, topless, and Mane watched as the scales that formed the skirt around her lower half folded into her body. Kit lay naked before him, her lips stained with blood. It was as if she could read his mind. "Will this help you to decide?"

"Are you sure?" Mane could barely hear himself speak. His heart pounded fiercely in his chest. His gaze was transfixed by her beautiful porcelain skin and the thin rivulet of blood that ran down her chin and between her breasts.

"Very sure."

It was all he needed. Mane loosened the ties of his pants and let them slide off as he closed the distance between them. He pressed his tongue to the end of the stream of blood, pulling upwards between her breasts and up the side of her neck. Kit groaned beneath him as he nibbled slightly at the ends of her earlobes.

"I feel as if I want to take you and bite you at the same time." Kit's words came out in a breathless pant.

Mane chuckled and sat back on his heels. "You can take me, but you'll never be able to bite me."

Kit sobered briefly. "Why is that?"

"I told you, I'm not from around here either. Most people, you will be able to harm. You just can't harm me."

"Good." Kit practically purred as she put her hand to the nape of Mane's neck and pulled him down, her voice coming out in a seductive whisper. "You're saying that if I want to rip someone's throat out, I can fuck you instead."

"If you have already gotten to the point of needing to rip someone's throat out you may be beyond the point where you can control the bloodlust." Mane ran his hand up Kit's bare thigh, parting it slightly. "But if you start to feel the pull..." He bent down closer to her. "A pulsing deep within which makes each sight and sound swirl around you until the hunger is all you can think about, then yes, you can fuck me all you like." Their eyes locked, and the fuse between them was lit. "Starting now."

Kit screamed out, a mix of pain and pleasure, as Mane thrust himself inside her. Mane's demon had decided there would be no gentle first time for Kit, but he had a feeling she didn't mind.

The chill of the night air couldn't penetrate their burning passion. Whenever Mane drew back, Kit pulled him closer. Only when their bodies were slick with sweat, their breath ragged, did Kit allow Mane to finally collapse to the ground. Both of them were thoroughly satiated to the point that he was pretty certain even if they were to encounter a river of luscious blood laced with cinnabar they would both be able to resist it.

"Are you okay?" Mane brushed a lock of Kit's blue hair behind her ear. Her glossy eyes stared up into the night sky and the stars overhead.

"I never imagined that the sky would look so much the same as on Earth."

"The Realms and Earth share the same sky. They just view it from opposite sides of the glass."

"So does that mean we share the same Gods?"

Mane let out a snort. "Every being on Earth thinks he knows who the Gods are. Every being in the Realms thinks he knows who the Gods are. I say the Gods are merely another set of beings like us looking through the glass at another angle, one which allows them to see more than we can see."

"They appear to be omnipotent when really they only have an unfair advantage?"

"I knew I liked you from the moment I saw you fall over reaching for that asphodel fruit, almost causing me to be speared by the selkies."

Kit clamped her hand over her mouth. "Oh no. I have to get back soon. Mother only let me go because she thought...she wanted me to..." Kit dropped her head and refused to finish her sentence.

"What is it, Kit? Can I help?"

"You have already helped enough." She returned her blue-green gaze to his eyes. "You've done more than I ever would have dreamed."

Now it was Mane's turn to blush. "It was all my pleasure." He wound a strand of her hair around his finger. "I almost feel as if I took advantage of you."

"No, if anyone did that it was me. And I would believe it was all my doing if my glamour worked on you." Kit rubbed her thumb absently over the amulet at her neck. "You know you are practically perfect for me. I have no intention of dating one of those awful selkies. Besides, I think we are all related somehow." Kit shivered. "Ick. So what do you say?"

Her bubbly demeanor was infectious. Mane felt a smile cross his lips, mirroring hers. "You want us to start 'dating'?"

Mane cocked his head to the side, trying to remember what dating entailed.

"You know, go steady, be my boyfriend, or what you do before you get married like Valora and Dooley." The scales around Kit formed into a skirt, and she quickly found her shirt and slid it over her head.

"You want me to be your mate." The thought popped into Mane's head and then quickly made its way to a place of permanence in his mind. Yes, this was what he wanted, too. Now he really needed to see what was in Mavrovo. Before, he wanted to see for his own selfish desires, now Kit's life could be at stake if what he feared was true.

Kit nodded. "I have a small problem. My mom expects me to return with an elf for her to eat. You're the only elf anywhere near here. See my dilemma?" She held her hands out, weighing them in the air.

Kit's problem had just become Mane's solution. "No trouble at all, my love. Your mother won't be able to do me any harm either. If you want, I can escort you home. I would love a chance to see where you live."

Kit produced the small vial of potion from the folds of her scales. "If you drink this you'll be able to breathe, but I don't know for how long."

"Well then, bottoms up."

CHAPTER FIVE

Mane took the potion all in one mouthful. Kit's gaze traveled down the sculpted muscles of his chest. She tried to keep her mind off what just happened, but Mane standing there shirtless wasn't helping matters. The murderous thoughts within her mind were locked up tight. Being with Mane had helped her control the bloodlust. But for how long? Of course, she could always tell him it was wearing off. It was great not being a kid anymore.

There was still the problem of Kit being a selkie and Mane being an elf. How would it ever work? Mane reached his hand out to Kit. "Let's go, I can feel the potion taking hold and I'll need to be in the water soon or I won't be able to breathe the air."

Kit took Mane's hand in hers and stepped towards the portal. The amulet at her neck flared blue, and white light from the portal lit up the night sky. They walked through, the waters of Mavrovo flooding in around Kit. She took in a deep breath and looked back at Mane.

He pawed at the water in front of him as if he couldn't quite believe that he was able to breathe. "Are you okay?"

Mane reached his hand to his throat. "Yes." He laughed. "Yes, this is unbelievable." His face turned serious as he surveyed the area around them.

They had come in the middle of the night which was a very busy time for the selkie. They weren't too far from the castle, but nobody had noticed them yet. That wouldn't last long. Kit wasn't sure how, but her mother always seemed to know where she was. It probably had to do with the amulet. Kit looked around and saw a forked firebush whose red bulbs seemed to glow even more red than usual since the cracks had opened up around the castle. Kit removed her amulet and shoved it into the plant, making sure that the chain was secure around the base so it wouldn't float away.

Kit looked up at Mane who hadn't moved and was staring at the castle. "It's pretty fantastic. But wait until you see the inside."

Mane was shaken from his reverie. "You want to bring me inside the castle? Isn't that dangerous?"

"Kind of exciting, isn't it? You said my mother couldn't hurt you, right?" Kit wanted to find a way to keep Mane down here longer. If she could get him more of the potion he would be able to breathe; however, steering clear of her mother would be a challenge. "Follow me."

Kit pulled at Mane's arm. He swam alongside her as they approached the castle gates. Two of her mother's guards were standing watch. "What is this? Lunch?" One of the guards bared his teeth and swam forwards.

Kit put her hand up. "My mother wanted me to bring the elf directly to her. Where is she?"

The guard stopped and crossed his arms over his chest. The other came up behind him. He was using the bone of some animal to pick at his sharpened teeth. Kit was glad she only had to deal with pointed canines.

The guard with the bone spoke first. "She is inside in her chambers."

"Okay, good, we'll go right there." Kit pulled Mane behind her. He seemed to be doing a fine job of acting all glassy eyed glamoured. He transfixed his gaze on the cracks surrounding the castle which were spewing the red ash into the water.

Kit quickly pressed her back against the wall as she looked down the corridor towards her mother's chambers. "We need to get across and down the other hall, but I don't want them to see us." A quick glance from where they had come revealed that the guards hadn't moved. They were standing at the entrance to the castle still busily picking at their teeth with the remnants of whatever had been their lunch. Kit felt Mane's hand on her shoulder. She turned and gasped as his eyes flared red.

"What's wrong with your eyes?"

Mane squeezed his eyes tight and shook his head, looking down at his feet before looking back up at Kit. The glow had faded, but it was certainly still present. "I don't mean to alarm you. I'll be okay. It's the cinnabar. It's really strong down here. How long has it been bleeding into the waters of Mavrovo?"

"Oh, you mean that red stuff? I asked my mother about that. She didn't want to talk about it. I think it only started last week. I hadn't noticed it before. But it seems to be increasing. No one pays much attention to it though. It's strange."

"They probably can't see it." Mane darted his gaze down the tunnel and towards Kit again. "We have to get somewhere safe. We are too exposed out here."

"I know." Kit heard the click of a door opening down the hall. *Her mother!* She glanced across the way to a door which she didn't remember going into before. "We need to hide." She pushed open the door. Mane followed behind her. The room they were in was pitch dark. Kit kept the door open a crack and watched as her mother came down the hall.

"She is out there. Have you two not seen her?" she bellowed.

The guards looked around, scratching their heads in confusion. "She was here a moment ago with an elf. I saw her go down the hall towards your chambers, Queen Elemi."

"Have you been drinking from the waters again? She can't be here. I sense her presence outside the castle gates. Near the portal entrance. Come with me." Elemi and the guards shot outside the door. So Kit had been right, her mother could track her with the amulet. Of course without the amulet she also couldn't leave Mavrovo. At least that was what her mother had told her.

A flicker of light in the corner of her eye caught her attention. She turned. Mane held his arm outstretched. A burst of flame rose from the center of his palm and illuminated a short distance ahead.

"How did you do that?"

The slight red tint to Mane's eyes glowed in the dim light. "Magic."

There was so much about the Realms that Kit didn't know about. Magic was as acceptable as anything else at the moment. And the other thing she didn't know about was this room.

"I would rather have had one of those for my birthday than these." Kit grabbed her chest. Her mother had obviously been holding out on her.

"I never would have guessed your mother was a gear head."

෪๛

49

Mane lifted his hand up higher. The light from the small flame erupting from the center of his palm bounced off the mirrored surfaces surrounding the upper portion of the room, reflecting down on the contents of the open space. There were about ten vehicles in the room. Kit blasted past Mane, taking off towards the shiny red number with the word "Porsche" on the side.

"Is this what you had wanted to show me?" Mane caught up with Kit and leaned on the open door of the car. A slight hum buzzed through his body, a side effect of the enchantment that had been put on the vehicles.

Kit settled down into the bucket seat and ran her hands along the leather. "I had no idea these were here. How can they still look brand new sitting underwater?"

"It is strange. I mean without feet I am not sure how your mother was planning on driving these things. But they are humming with magic. She certainly has some plans for them."

A flash of black and red caught Mane's attention. He reached down and took Kit by the wrist. "Come and see this one."

Kit giggled as Mane raced over and slid his hand across the hood of the shiny black vehicle.

"What kind of car is that?"

Mane laughed. "One you probably have never heard of." He bent down, admiring the vertical grill before pulling open the door. "After you, my darling. Meet Edsel."

Kit slid into the driver's seat and scooted over to the passenger side as Mane eased himself gently into the driver's side. "How do you know about cars? You're an elf."

"I've lived a long time. I was in Chicago during the 1950s. This car is just like the one I had. It's amazing." Mane ran his hands along the red leather of the steering wheel. He couldn't forget the Edsel. He gripped his head as his demon pounded against the confines of its fleshy prison. It was then that he had been free of anyone's control -- before he had renounced Ravanna. How was it possible that Elemi could have this car here in her garage? "I mean, look at the rolling dome speedometer and the Push-button Teletouch transmission."

Mane paused, his finger twitching above the button that opened the glove compartment. If they were still in there, then it would confirm his suspicions. He wasn't sure what it would mean or if revisiting his past was a smart idea.

He had to know. The small indentations in the leather grip around the steering wheel fit Mane's hands perfectly. "Kit, can you please do me a favor and open that? Tell me what's inside."

Mane stared forward out the window, looking at the other cars that Elemi stored in her garage. They were from a wide range of eras, all with the polish and shine of a brand new car. But they weren't all new if Kit found in the glove box what he thought she would find.

The compartment opened with a click, and Kit gave a squeal. "They are so cool! How do I look?"

She tipped her head and gave him a naughty stare over the tops of a pair of red cat eye sunglasses with small white rhinestones at the tips. His breath caught in his throat. Kit's hair faded into a golden brown as Mane was drawn into that moment in Chicago in 1958. She smiled coyly, the darkened shades hiding the brilliant green of her eyes. Catherine never knew that it was the last time she would ever look at him that way.

"Beautiful."

"Is everything okay? I'm not working my mojo on you by accident, am I?" She took off the glasses and examined them. "Wait, the lenses are dark. You can't see my eyes anyway with them on. These will come in handy." She placed the glasses back on her face and he was bespelled once more.

Mane pulled her onto his lap in the small space between his chest and the steering wheel, but he wanted her closer. Needed her closer.

"So beautiful." Mane pressed his mouth against the fabric of her shirt and tugged at it with his teeth. If it wasn't her only one he would have ripped it right off.

Kit brushed the frame of her glasses with her fingertips as Mane snaked his hands under her shirt.

"No, keep the glasses on."

"As long as I can take the shirt off, I'll leave the glasses on." Kit caressed Mane's muscled arms, encouraging him with her movements as he pushed her shirt up and pressed his face into her chest, gently grazing her nipples with the edges of his teeth.

"You are driving me crazy," he mumbled into her.

"I think you are the one in the driver's seat." Kit looked down at her lower half, which was currently a pair of fins. "Don't think that we'll be doing much down here."

Mane laughed. "You can control that. You produced a skirt for yourself when you were on land. Why can't you produce legs now?"

"I suppose you're right." Kit's fins unknit into legs and the heat between them caused a physical response in Mane that made his clothing uncomfortable. She pushed herself off Mane's lap and finished taking off her shirt. "It's not quite fair that I'm naked, and you're wearing all those clothes."

"I've only got on shorts."

"Still, not fair." Kit crossed her arms over her chest and gave a fake pout.

"Then why don't you take them off for me?"

Kit reached over and undid the tie at the top of Mane's shorts. She pulled them down and gasped. Having sex in the dark hadn't given her a chance to see how he measured up. But now, in his excited state, she saw that he had something to brag about.

"No wonder that hurt before."

"It won't hurt so much next time. You'll get used to it." Mane gave a wicked grin and leaned over towards her.

"No, wait." She trailed her finger across the crease between his hip and his inner thigh before dipping her head down to trace the same path with a row of delicate kisses.

Mane leaned his head back on the seat and closed his eyes. He moaned in pleasure as Kit took him between her soft lips.

Kit paused. "Is this okay?" Mane could feel the demon rising within him. He didn't need to look in the mirror to see that his eyes were most likely glowing red now.

"Don't stop." Mane heard his voice come out in a sharp rasp. Damn, this selkie was undoing every last bit of his resolve.

Kit pushed her glasses onto her nose and touched her tongue lightly to his exposed flesh. It was more than Mane could handle. He pulled her up in one swift movement and brought her onto his lap, his engorged length pressing into her with ease. There was definitely an advantage to doing this underwater. The only disadvantage was that he couldn't smell Kit's scent or feel her sweat against his skin. And it was her that he wanted, not the memory of his Catherine. He had given up on her long ago and never looked back.

Mane wanted to do more than feel his own release. He rubbed his thumb against the swollen nub between her legs and her body clamped down even tighter on him. She held onto his shoulders and thrust her head back as they both rode the wave of pleasure all the way to the end.

It was about that time that he heard the click of the door. The overhead lights flicked on one by one, the last throwing a spotlight on their naked bodies in a highly compromising position in the front seat of the Edsel.

Kit jumped off Mane, throwing her shirt on as her legs knit together again.

"Where do we hide?" asked Kit.

"I'm not sure we can." Mane pulled his shorts on, silently cursing himself for letting Kit weave her magic on him. She might not have any real power over him, but she didn't need it. He was head over heels for this one.

Mane turned and saw Kit's mother enter the room flanked by the two guards. Queen Elemi peered into the window of each car as she walked down the row. She had Kit's amulet in her hand, and she didn't look happy.

Mane caught Kit by the shoulders and forced her to look at him. "They are going to be here any second. I can get out of here, but you need to stay."

"How are you going to get out of here?" Kit's lips trembled.

"This." Mane ran his hand along the dash of the Edsel.

"You're going to drive it out of here?"

"This is not only like the car I used to have. Kit, it is the car I used to have. I can't explain. But it wouldn't do you any good to come with me."

"Yes, and I can't because my mom has the amulet I need to be out of Mavrovo."

Mane put his hand to her chin and forced her to look at him once more. "I will return for you, I promise. There are things I want to tell you. We can continue our lessons. You are supposed to attend the wedding in a few weeks, and you have much to learn."

"I'll be more than happy to have more lessons from you." Kit briefly pressed against the bulge in Mane's pants. "I'll try to reach you tomorrow. But I don't know how or when."

Mane clenched his jaw as he tried to shake off the rise she brought forth in him. It still seemed surreal that he had found another woman who could do that so naturally. Catherine was the first, and he'd thought she would be the last. "That's okay. We have bonded. Your blood calls to me. We will find each other."

Kit gave an easy nod before running her hand down his muscled chest. Confidently, she exited the car. She trusted him. He beat down the strong desire within him to follow her, to protect her.

๛

"What are you doing in here? I have been looking all over for you. Where is that elf you were supposed to bring me?" Elemi's temper was apparent in the forceful current of her words which crossed the room with ease.

Just then a brilliant glow surrounded the Edsel. It rose about a foot in the air and a portal opened underneath it. As quickly as that happened, the Edsel disappeared.

Elemi rushed to Kit. "What kind of demon did you let in here?"

"There was no demon. Only that elf. I was trying to keep him occupied. I had no idea these cars were even here, let alone that they conjured portals." Kit pushed her fists into her hips.

"They don't. They only open portals for me and for demons. So explain to me again how this happened."

Kit clamped her hand over her mouth. If the car only

worked for her mother and for demons that meant Mane was a demon.

Her father was going to kill her.

CHAPTER SIX

Mane let go of the breath he was holding and sucked in the scorched air. His shorts dried in an instant under the hot sun of the Ordos desert. The potion Kit gave him wore off seconds before he was able to get the car to portal out of there. He was glad that he was right and that this was the car that Ravanna had used to send him Earthside when he was still running missions for the demon king. If Elemi had the car it certainly meant her dealings with Ravanna were real. He didn't give away his magic easily.

Mane patted the dash. "Nice to see you again, old girl. Time for me to take you on a spin through my new neighborhood. Quite a bit different than Chicago."

Mane revved the engine of the car which had been spelled by Ravanna and no longer needed gas in the tank. It only required a demon at the wheel, and Mane was all too happy to oblige. Back when he had garnered favor with the demon king he had been sent to Chicago to retrieve a shifter that owed Ravanna a debt. The year was 1958, and he could never have guessed that he would fall for Catherine and Ravanna would use his moment of weakness against him.

Kit had certainly grown into her skin. She looked so much like Catherine. He didn't realize how much until she slipped on Catherine's red cat eye glasses which were in the same place she last left them, in the glove box of Mane's car right before the demon king claimed her for his own. Humans did not stay human when they were pulled down to Acheron. They became something else entirely. So for all intents and purposes Catherine was dead. Ravanna should not have been surprised that Mane not only disagreed with his plan to expand onto Earth, but laughed at his plan to do so. That defiance had killed Catherine and gotten Mane banished. Banished into the body of an elf in the Realms.

Now Kit had been placed in his path, and he wasn't going to let her go. She needed his help as Catherine once did. He had no intention of letting Ravanna ruin his chance to be happy with his half-selkie, half-human protégé. However, he was going to have to figure out how to get past the fact that she could only survive in the waters of Mavrovo and that his true home was in a realm he would make sure she never entered.

The edge of the Riparian forest came into view. The Edsel was like a black bullet speeding across the dry desert sands. A place without life. The only place he could portal into since he was a demon. He avoided portal travel unless he was in a group where he knew others would be able to open the portal to the Riparian. Each being in the Realms could naturally open portals to their birthplace once taught the right magic. As a demon, his birthplace wasn't even in this realm. So he was spit out into the dry deserts of the Ordos, known by the locals as Dragonlands for the only other creatures who would even venture here. It was a funny coincidence that the dragons, whom those of the Realms believed to be the creatures of the Goddess Varuna, would choose the only place he, a demon, could portal into.

Of course, there was more of a connection between the Goddess and the demon king than anyone in the Realms knew. Mane wasn't worried about it as long as they both stayed where they belonged. Then there was no quarrel. Unfortunately, what he had seen in Mavrovo showed him that Ravanna was no longer happy staying where he was.

Mane adjusted the mirror and took a look at his reflection, his eyes swirling with anger the color of the deep red leather seats of the Edsel. He hadn't been home in a while. He hoped that he would be welcome at his homecoming and not shoved on a hot stake above a roaring fire. He had hidden his demon nature from them, but he slipped a lot lately and he wasn't ready to give up his disguise yet.

He had no desire to face Ravanna on his territory. Ravanna would win. He could only hope to keep Ravanna where he was and himself in this body.

Mane pulled the Edsel into the shade of the trees that lined the Riparian. It was as far as he dared take it. He covered it with branches to hide its reflective surfaces from passing dragons that would be entering the skies soon. Evening was falling, and the night was the dominion of the beast. That and many others.

Mane gave a wink to the Cyclops eye that graced the grill of the Edsel. "I'll be back for you, babe." A promise he had also given Kit. A promise he wasn't sure how he was going to keep. A promise that relied on her being able to find her way out of Mavrovo with her amulet.

❧

Kit sat in her chambers for an eternity. When the door opened she jumped, expecting her mother to blast in and punish her for trespassing in her garage of collectibles and for bringing Mane, who was apparently a demon, inside the castle. Instead, it was Kit's father, Ralph.

He was at her side in an instant and threw his arms around her. "I can't believe how much you have grown. Your mother tried to warn me, but I had no idea. Are you okay?"

Ralph's eyes were full of concern. It was as if he forgot that he was present when she fell into the selkie sleep and that, even though he had promised he would be there when she woke up, he had been gone.

"Yeah, Dad, I'm fine. It was a bit of a shock at first, but I suppose my instinct to live has kicked in and I'm fine now. Just trying to catch my mind up with my body." She didn't realize that was how she felt until the words left her mouth. She could never lie to her father. Apparently she could lie to herself, but not to her father.

Kit flopped into her father's arms, her tears blending with the surrounding water. Her mother had told her selkie didn't cry, and Mavrovo seemed to agree.

After she had finished sobbing she looked up into her father's face. "It's not safe for us here, Daddy. We must leave."

Ralph shook his head. "You can't leave, Kit. The waters of Mavrovo are what allow you to survive."

Kit looked down at the amulet which once again hung at her neck. "Mother tells me that I need the waters, but who is to say that is true, Dad? This amulet allows me to be outside the waters longer than any other selkie."

"That and the fact that you are half-human." Looking back at her father, a human who had sacrificed his entire life for her, Kit couldn't help but feel selfish. She wanted to escape her mother, but whatever she did, her mother would still have a hold over her father. If she permanently left Mavrovo, she would take her father with her. But the selkie would never let her leave. Her mother would never let her leave. Only if all of the selkie were dead would she be free.

"I'll never forget that, Dad." She looked up at the familiar creases on the sides of his eyes. Wrinkles from all the moments they had laughed together. He could always make her laugh. "I wish you and I could go fishing again."

Ralph chuckled. "I think fishing is the last thing your mother would let me do." He cradled Kit's face in his hands. "My dear daughter, I know adjusting to life down here is difficult, but you can do it. We can do it. Together." He placed a kiss on her forehead and dropped his hands to his side. His loving demeanor became serious in an instant. "What is this I hear about you bringing a demon into the castle?"

"Did mother put you up to this?" Kit had expected to have trouble with her father when it came to boys, considering he used to be the town sheriff. But this was ridiculous.

"She told me what happened. But, no, she did not."

"I had no idea he was a demon. This is news to me, too."

"Then I assume you will steer clear of him in the future?" Ralph tipped his head, looking at her and knowing she could give nothing but an honest answer.

"Yes, Daddy, I will." It wasn't true, of course. She had just lied to her father. There was a first time for everything.

Ralph nodded and opened the door to exit Kit's room. Kit started to relax at the door, but the instant it was open her mother appeared.

She gave Ralph a quick peck on the lips and pushed him out the door as she shut it behind her.

"You may have been able to fool your father into believing you had no idea who that demon was, but you won't fool me so easily." Elemi's teeth looked extra sharp today for some reason. She was vicious. Kit wondered what purpose she served to Elemi. Why she had ever been allowed here in the first place?

"Mom, I had no idea. All I knew was that he was an elf and he was helping me learn to adjust."

"Learn to adjust!" Elemi pushed her finger into Kit's chest. "Anything you need to learn will come from your people. These feelings you have are natural. They are the normal desire, the normal hunger of a selkie. You shouldn't need to adjust to anything."

"But I killed an elf, Mom."

"So? If an elf got close enough to the banks of Mavrovo it probably had a death wish. It is our nature to hunt those weaker than us, darling. And all of the creatures of the Realms are weaker than us."

"I don't believe that." Kit knew Valora, a fae of Dell'Aria, and she had known Franca, a dwarf from Mount Elbrus, before she was killed. The last thing she thought of when she thought of those two was weakness. And Mane was anything but weak.

"Really? You let loose your demon when you slayed that elf. Nothing could have stopped you. It is that force within us which makes us the most powerful. The only thing that holds us back is our tether to the waters." Elemi reached out and stroked Kit's long blue tresses with her hand. "Kit, you have the ability to walk on the surface of the Realms. No one else has that. The fact that you so easily slayed an elf without any training shows me your true potential. Proves to me that my dealings with Ravanna will give us our rightful place in the Realms."

"And what place is that?" Kit knew she was playing with fire, but she wanted to know Elemi's plan.

"A place where we can hunt freely. Where we are not forced to eat only the sea creatures and the few beings that wander near the banks. Where I don't have to venture through the portals to Earth to find my next meal."

"So you were going to eat Dad?"

"The thought had crossed my mind. However, I realized that your father could provide me with a child. A child which might hold the key to freedom for the selkie." Elemi perched on the side of the bed next to Kit. "You are a blessing to us all, Kit. You will lead the selkie into a new age after I am gone, an age where we will be free of our watery prison."

"I thought you enjoyed the waters. It's a good place for the selkie. If they were free to roam, wouldn't they destroy everything in their path?"

Elemi rose again. "If that is what comes to pass than it is what's meant to be. It won't be long before we find out. But you must stay away from that elf. I don't know what it wants, but my deal is with Ravanna, not with any lesser demon."

"Your deal?"

"Yes, one which will truly set us free."

Elemi swept out of the room. Kit clutched the amulet to her chest and curled up on her bed. "My father taught me that nothing in life is ever free. I'm sure the same applies in the Realms."

One thing was for certain. She needed to find Mane, and she needed an explanation. Was he on her mother's side or on his own? He certainly hadn't told her anything about being a demon.

CHAPTER SEVEN

Mane passed through the shimmering wall of magic that surrounded his camp. It bubbled around him becoming visible as he passed through it and then returning invisible again. That was a telling sign. The wards hadn't been changed to keep him out, so he wasn't considered a threat.

Or maybe it was because everyone was gone. Mane bent down to the remains of a smoldering fire and held his hand above the embers. There was barely any heat left. His tribe had moved on without him. Mane rushed towards the inner circle of camp and froze when he saw his family's tent still standing. Hanging at the entrance, the bells of the trinket the shaman had made to ward off the evil spirits he said were attacking his father still tinkled in the slight breeze.

Slowly he approached the entrance and put his head in. His father lay on the bed, the shallow rise and fall of his chest barely visible. Mane rushed to his side and collected his hand which lay limp outside the blanket placed over him.

"Father, what has happened? Where is everyone?"

His father's eyes parted ever so slightly. His chest rattled as he tried to take a deeper breath. "They have left. I ordered them all to go. Even your mother and sister. They need to find a place where there is food. There is nothing here for us anymore."

"But they left you behind." Mane put his hand to his father's forehead expecting the heat of the fever that usually wracked his body and made him ill, but there was only coldness. Too cold.

"My time has come to join the Elysium. There was no need for them to transport my body. No need."

Mane rubbed his father's cold hand between his which felt hot in comparison. "There is so much I want to thank you for. So much I never got a chance to say." The man had been a father to Mane for so many cycles in the Realms. Mane had lived more lifetimes than anyone in the Realms, but he never had a chance to have a father. Now he had to say goodbye to this man whom he would never see again. His father would, without a doubt, be granted entrance to the Elysium, a place Mane would never be allowed as a demon of the Acheron. Although he could pass between the Realms and other parallel worlds, Elysium was the one place he would never gain entrance to, an arrangement it looked as though Ravanna was trying to change.

"I know this is our final goodbye, son. I know you cannot follow me where I go. I think I might have a talk with the elders at Elysium, see if I can change that."

"How do you know?"

"I have always known. Even when you were born I was near the end of my life. Elves can see through the veil at the end of their life cycles. I saw the Soulstealer take my son's soul and shove yours inside. You seemed none too happy about it. I did my best to raise you so that you would see that there is another way in life."

"You did that, Father. I wish there was some way I

could repay you for all you have done for me."

Mane's father gestured towards a box which lay on the top of a chest near his feet. All his life he had been told it was off limits. "Take the box, bring it here."

He placed the box on his father's chest. "Help me sit up."

Mane stood behind his father, placing his hands under his arms and gently pulling him up to a seated position. He propped several pillows behind him for support. Mane's father opened the box and pulled out a small roll of vellum covered in black lettering. "I sought this out when you were born. When I was afraid. Before I knew who you were." Mane reached out and accepted the vellum that his father handed to him.

"What is it for?"

"It is for banishing the demon from this Realm. I do not know how long it will last. But it should hold him off long enough for you to find another way that is more permanent."

"Why didn't you use it?"

"Because I was afraid it might cause you harm." He paused and reached out, the thin skin of his hand like a feather on Mane's shoulder. "I saw into your soul. You've been tortured long enough."

"But demons don't have souls."

"You do."

It was the last words Mane's father ever said to him. Mane set the vellum into the box and placed it to the side before gently returning his father to a resting position. His final resting position.

"May the gates of Elysium open wide for you, Father. You certainly deserve a king's welcome."

King. Now that his father was dead the title passed

straight onto him. Mane opened the chest and looked at the vellum through blurred eyes. The writing called for a ceremony. He would gather the elves together in ritual. A sacred ritual that he could easily tack onto that which would be called for in his father's passing. He needed to catch up with his tribe. But first he had to find Kit. Before he performed this ritual, he would make sure she was nowhere near Mavrovo when it happened.

If he was correct the cracks that Elemi had somehow managed to conjure between the Realms and Acheron would be sealed, making it more difficult for Ravanna to find his way through. It was a temporary fix, but anything was better than nothing right now.

෨ᦉ

Kit waited patiently for the night to turn to day. She sucked in a deep breath as the light began to shine down through the waters, casting a shimmer above her head. Her mother had gone down for her daytime rest as had the other selkie. She was the only one who did not succumb to sleep when the sun reached the sky. Her mother said Kit would guide the selkie into another age. One where she was the ruler. Who was to say that they wouldn't kill her in her sleep?

Elemi had struck some kind of deal with the demon king Ravanna. The cinnabar that bled red into the waters of Mavrovo was somehow related. It wasn't enough to stain the waters, but it seemed to increase a little every day, and with the increase in the cinnabar came an increase in the violent temperament of the selkie, including herself. Leaving now would be the only way to save any humanity she had left. She had to convince her mother to agree to let her go.

She reached into her pocket and pulled out the invitation that Mane had given to her. Valora's wedding to Dooley was

67

only a week away. She could convince her mother that Valora needed her at Winter Haven to help her prepare for the ceremony. Maybe Valora or the priests could help her. But she didn't want to ask and start a war between her mother and Valora's father on her wedding day.

Getting away from Mavrovo would give her a chance to really think. A chance to clear the cinnabar from her system and reflect on everything that had happened. Kit slid on the red cat eye sunglasses and fussed a bit with her blue locks in the mirror. First, she had to find Mane.

Kit walked past the door to the room that she and Mane had stumbled upon. All those cars. Apparently they could be used as portals, but what a strange thing. Kit opened the door and looked inside. A single light shone down upon the black Edsel. It had returned to the garage, but Mane wasn't inside.

A tapping on her shoulder caused Kit to jump. She whirled around and faced down one of Elemi's two guards. "Looking for your boyfriend?"

"No." Kit slammed the door behind her and tried to push past the guard towards her mother's room.

"Where do you think you're going?" The guard's grip on Kit's shoulder tightened to the point of pain, but she refused to yell out and show him how he was affecting her.

"To see my mother. I am sure she wouldn't want you to stop me from seeing her."

The guard's eyes flashed red. "I'll make sure you get there okay."

Damn. Kit was going to have to figure out another plan. Sneaking past her mother was no longer an option. She wracked her brain as the guard escorted her down the hall. She was going to have to think of a really good reason for waking her mother and for leaving Mavrovo again.

Kit knocked at the door, and it opened of its own accord. "There better be a good reason for waking me from my sleep." Elemi's voice came from within the darkened room.

The guard spoke first. "Your daughter wanted to see you."

"Send her in."

The guard gave Kit a shove and closed the door behind her. Kit was in the dark and her mother, Queen Elemi, was somewhere in the room. She had awakened her mother during the middle of her day sleep. A warm pulse of water hot against her neck signaled her mother's presence before she had said a word.

"Tell me why you have awakened me, daughter. It must be important. You do know that although you are half-selkie your human side smells quite delightful to me at the moment. The sleep is the only thing that staves off the hunger. That is, until we awaken."

Kit clasped her hands in front of her, silently saying an unknown prayer to an unknown god. When she was young she often went hunting and fishing with her father on Cougar Mountain, given its name because it was home to the beast. He had taught her to make noises as they walked down the trail in order to scare off the predator and also what to do if she came face to face with him. Kit stayed still. The last thing she needed to do was to panic and cause her own mother's predatory nature to strike her down as part of the chase.

Kit slowly reached into her pocket and pulled out the invitation. "I wanted to talk to you about going to Winter Haven."

This must have struck her mother as funny because she began to laugh out loud, and a small glow erupted from the lamp at her bedside. It never ceased to amaze Kit that this magical light could exist even underwater.

"You want to float amongst the clouds at Winter Haven? My dear daughter, I doubt the priests would ever allow you to be so close to their precious Goddess."

Kit handed the paper to her mother. "A fae priest delivered this to me inviting me there. Well, delivered it to Mane to give to me."

The paper puckered as Elemi clutched it tightly. "A priest gave this invitation to a demon to deliver to you? There must be more to this demon than I thought. Interesting. When do you propose to go?"

Kit's eyebrows rose. She was unable to hide her amazement at the fact that her mother was so suddenly agreeable. "I was hoping to go right away. I thought maybe Valora could use my help preparing for the ceremony. Maybe I could throw her a bachelorette party."

Elemi put a finger to her chin. "I don't think I can make the appropriate arrangements for me to depart so soon. There is potion to be prepared."

"What do you mean?"

"Well, I'm going with you, of course. You don't think I would allow you to go on your own."

"But the invitation was to me. I..."

Elemi cut her off. "Dear daughter, the priest should know that if he has invited you, he has invited me. Very well, you go ahead of me and announce our arrival. I will be there for the ceremony. I have an interest in Winter Haven and Valora. It is a wonderful idea."

Kit started to exit the room. She wasn't sure if she had done the right thing. She turned back towards her mother. "You'll bring father along, right?"

"Of course. They would probably be suspicious if I

didn't. Plus, I think your father needs to dry out. The potions we have given him seem to be affecting his memory a bit. And one more thing, darling. Make sure you feed before you leave. You don't want to be chomping on the wedding guests. At least not until I get there." Elemi laughed, and Kit gave an uncomfortable chuckle.

Kit shut the door to her mother's room. What had she done? She wanted to escape. Now she had given her mother the chance at a fae buffet. The only way she could keep that from happening was to attend the wedding. Valora didn't need to know all the gritty details. Valora could keep her wedding day, and Kit could escape the waters. Hopefully things would work out for both of them.

Kit swam past the guards and outside the castle gates. None of them followed her. She wasn't sure what Mane wanted from her. Maybe he had used her to get to that car in her mother's castle. He was a demon and had said nothing to her about it. She wasn't sure who to trust anymore. Maybe she couldn't trust anyone.

When she crested the surface of Mavrovo, he was standing there on the banks. Locating Mane wasn't going to be a problem. He had found her.

CHAPTER EIGHT

Mane reached the banks as she crested the water. The gentle ripples of magic that tickled his thighs told him she was coming. Kit was strong with magic, stronger than she knew, and Mane was attuned to it.

They looked at one another. Neither moving from their position. Mane wanted to give her the chance to come to him even though her pull on him made him want to dive in after her. But he knew it wasn't magic. Her powers at glamour had no effect on him. And she could never hurt him with her bite. He also would not be able to hurt her. He hadn't meant to hurt Catherine. Mane felt a pull on his soul, the one he thought he didn't have, but his father said he did. He knew that if he lost Kit there was no other purpose for him here in the Realms. He would wither and die and be born anew into another body, another soul to be stolen, because Ravanna had permanently banished him from Acheron. Not that he wanted to return, but he wished he had the power to stop Ravanna. To keep Kit and the Realms safe.

Mane's heart pounded in his chest. Sweat broke out on

his brow as the sun beat down on him. Kit continued to wade just outside the shallows. Seconds stretched into minutes and Mane couldn't take it anymore. He dove into the waters and swam out to Kit, stopping several feet away.

"You made it back."

Kit nodded but didn't say anything.

"I was hoping you would."

"Why? So you could use me like my mother does?" The hurt in her voice was obvious and the accusation seemed to come out of nowhere. Evidently her mother had revealed who he was. He should have known that the second he took the car his secret would be out.

"Kit, I knew that my true nature wasn't relevant when we first met. I saw in you what my father saw in me, someone with a strong soul despite the demons they were fighting, and I had an urge to help you." Mane dropped his head as he remembered the other reason why he had wanted to help Kit. "And to be honest, I did want you to take me to your castle, but only because I wanted to see what was happening with Mavrovo. The cinnabar is not usually this prevalent unless Ravanna is involved. I wanted to see what was happening."

"You've seen, and you know my mother has dealings with him. What is it you plan to do?"

She was giving him a chance to reveal his true intentions and he wasn't going to waste it. "Mavrovo is not safe for you anymore. Ravanna is coming. It is only a matter of time. I intend to perform a ritual that will seal the cracks for now and delay him, but it won't stop him. But more than all that, I wanted to protect you."

"Why would you want to do that?" She hid her true feelings behind those darkened glasses. Before he had wanted her to keep them on, now he wished she would take them off. He had no idea what the revelation of his being a demon would do to the two of them. It was the first time in a while that he actually felt vulnerable.

"Because I care about you. A lot."

Kit took the glasses off her face and propped them up on the top of her head. Her eyes were dry. She wasn't upset. "You're doing this all for me?"

Mane wanted more than anything to rush towards her and to prove that to her, but he didn't want to scare her away. "Yes."

"What about you being a demon? You know, my father isn't too excited about that." Her flirtatious tone warmed Mane's bones. He knew he wasn't going to lose her, but he still needed to choose his words carefully.

"I fight my demons every day, just as you do. And when I said you couldn't hurt me, I lied. If you left and I never saw you again that would absolutely destroy me." Mane watched as a smile played across Kit's face.

"I'm not going anywhere." She swam towards him and threw her arms around his neck, planting kisses on his forehead and cheeks. "You're going to seal the cracks? That's awesome!"

Kit drew away and looked into Mane's eyes. "After that what will happen?"

Mane couldn't help but trail his fingers down Kit's side. His hand came in contact with the soft scales which adorned her lower half, still in selkie form. A shiver passed through Kit's body. She inched close enough for her taut nipples to brush against the firm muscles of his chest.

Mane continued to let her dictate the moment. The last thing he wanted to do was to be overbearing, even though his baser needs were making him crazed with her so near. "I am not sure what will happen after that. My father has passed away. I am leader of my tribe, though they are on their way out of the Riparian to find another home. The elves know what is coming and don't want to be here when it happens."

"I'm so sorry to hear about your father. I hope what you are doing will help to save mine. Will you go with the other elves?"

"Not if I have a reason not to." Mane reached out and brushed his hand down the side of Kit's face. "I must catch up with the tribe to perform the ritual. After that, I intend to pass on the title to another."

Kit took Mane's hand and swam to shore. As she reached the shallows her legs unknit as she stepped from the waters and turned to face Mane in nothing but the short t-shirt which barely stretched over her breasts and the shimmering scales which adorned her lower half.

Mane's mouth ran dry at the sight of her. "Then let's run away together, Mane. Let's run away and never come back."

She reached her arms out to him, beckoning him onto the shore with her. Mane walked from the waters, loosening the tie on his shorts as he did so, easily stepping out of them and leaving them on the sand. His excitement was obvious as he approached her.

He reached down and pulled her shirt off. He barely grazed the tip of her hardened nipple with his thumb, eliciting another shiver which caused Kit's fangs to extend. She reached up and clasped her hand over her mouth.

"Oops." Mane moved her hand aside and rubbed the sharpened tooth with his finger, eliciting another sexual response from Kit. "It's okay. What we are about to do will stave off your hunger for the time being. Then we will hunt and find you some food. I will help you find a way to survive alongside your demons. I've had a lot of practice."

"Seems like you have had a lot of practice at quite a few things." Kit reached down and stroked Mane's stiff member. "I think I will have to stay after class for some extra credit."

"I'd be more than happy to oblige." Mane collected Kit in his arms and gently lowered her to the sand. Kit needed his form of help and needed it now. He braced his arms on either side of her hips, and she arched her back in response to his penetration. Her scales shimmered in the sunshine. Mane couldn't help but marvel at the beauty of her creamy skin. He dipped his head down and took her pink nipple into his mouth.

Kit screamed out, "Oh God, please don't stop."

Her eyes were closed, mouth open as she trembled beneath him. He held Kit tighter, anchoring his soul to her small form as he felt himself burst apart. His only tether was the love that he had for her.

❧❧

Kit's body continued to spasm as she rested in Mane's arms on the shores of Mavrovo. As they lay there, he explained to her how he came to live within the body of the elf. Mane's story was similar to hers. Even though she had been born a human, her selkie side had started to take over. It almost felt as though a part of her soul was missing. But Mane assured her it was still there. Funny enough, she felt most human in the arms of this demon.

"So you don't think that you should come to the wedding with me?" Kit trailed her fingers along Mane's smooth chiseled abdomen.

"I can't. The priest doesn't want me anywhere near your friend Valora."

"But I'll tell him that there isn't anything wrong with you. He'll listen to me."

"It's probably a good idea that I am not around your mother either. And I am pretty certain your father would not approve of me."

"He wouldn't approve of anyone. No one is good enough for his little girl. But I guess I will be busy with Valora and planning her bachelorette party."

"Do you really intend to give her such a thing? I know it is custom where you come from, but things are a bit different here in the Realms."

Kit rolled over and pressed her lips against Mane's. He quickly parted them and allowed her tongue to explore his, the tension in both of their bodies coming to a peak once more. "Not that different."

Mane laughed. "Why don't you bring her to the ritual? I will be able to see you for a bit, and I think it will provide Valora with the type of entertainment you're looking for."

Kit squealed with delight as Mane gave her the details of the ritual. "That's perfect! I should get going soon. I need to contact my mother once I get to Winter Haven so she knows I'm there. I'm not sure how they will react when I tell them about her arrival."

"I shall have you again in a fortnight."

Kit jumped up and pulled on her shirt, flipping open the red glasses and placing them on her face. "Yes, you will." She gave Mane one last kiss before jumping into Mavrovo to find the portal to Winter Haven.

∂∾∽

Mane pulled on his shorts and sat on the banks of Mavrovo, allowing the sun to beat down on his skin. He would have to leave soon to find his tribe, but he was having a hard time pulling himself away from the banks. A hard time believing that after all these years he had finally found someone like his Catherine. But better because Kit could not be influenced by Ravanna the same way Catherine was. At least as long as he performed the ritual and stopped the cinnabar from flooding Mavrovo. If that were to happen, all the selkie would become slaves to Ravanna's influence. He had no idea how it would affect Kit because she was half-human, and he had no intention of finding out.

Mane rose to leave when a shrieking sound blasted through the air above him. He looked up expecting to see a dragon, though that would be unusual in the middle of the day in this area of the Realms. What he saw instead was entirely unexpected. One of the airships that serviced the isles of Overworld, the realm of the fae, plunged down fast and hard from the sky, taking the clouds along with it.

Before it hit the center of the lake, he saw a figure jump off the side. Mavrovo seemed to know what to do with this foreign object. The waters reached up like the tendrils of some large sea creature and wrapped strong waves of waters across the bow and stern, pulling the ship down under with great force, but without destroying it.

As the last of the sails disappeared the surface of the water was still again. No debris floated to the surface. Then suddenly a head popped out and swam to the opposite bank.

Mane watched as the figure exited the water. It looked like a fae, a woman, but her wings were only a skeletal frame. She locked her gaze with Mane briefly before disappearing into the Riparian.

There were strange happenings in Mavrovo. The quicker Mane could find his tribe and perform the ritual the quicker he could be with Kit again and keep her safe from whatever it was.

Mane turned his attention to the sand, drawing the symbols that provoked the enchantment to direct him to the elves. He would bring word of his father's death and of his desire to perform the ritual to give up his claim to the title. He knew Torkel would accept the title, but he had no idea if the ritual would keep Ravanna at bay.

All he could do was try.

Thank you for reading *Mane Attraction*.

If you enjoyed *Mane Attraction*, please consider helping others to enjoy this book as well.

- **Recommend it.** Please help other readers find this book by recommending it to friends, readers groups, and discussion boards.

- **Review it.** Please tell other readers why you liked this book by reviewing it at one of the following websites: Amazon, Barnes and Noble, or Goodreads.

Mane Attraction is a novella set within the Realms, a world created for the Soulstealer Trilogy. If you like Mane and Kit's story and would like to see what happens with the ritual and with their steamy romance, you can read the continuation of their adventures in *Fae Guardian (The Soulstealer Trilogy, Book #2)*. If you missed the first book in the series, don't forget to check out *Fae Hunter (The Soulstealer Trilogy, Book #1)*.

FAE HUNTER (*The Soulstealer Trilogy, Book #1*)

Valora Delos is a Hunter, charged with tracking the treacherous Soulstealers and bringing them to justice. Unlike the other fae of her kind, Valora was born with stunted wings that render her flightless, driving her to prove herself in the eyes of King Aric, with whom she has been infatuated since she first set eyes on him as a young prince.

She descends to Earth and finds herself trapped in suburban Seattle after the portal to her world closes. With the help of a sexy half-fae named Dooley, Valora must find her way back to save Dell'Aria. Dooley uses his own brand of magic to help Valora discover memories buried deep within her, which produce more questions than answers- questions about her growing attraction to Dooley and her devotion to her King. Uncovering who the Soulstealers are and who is behind the destruction of Dell'Aria brings Valora a truth she may not be able to handle.

FAE GUARDIAN (*The Soulstealer Trilogy, Book #2*)

Dealing with wedding day woes, naked elven rituals, a best friend with a biting problem, dragon battles, and a war brewing between the selkie and the fae are only the beginning for Valora, the Fae Guardian.

Valora needs to get Aric out of her mind if she's going to live happily ever after with Dooley. But nothing is ever easy with magic. Tying herself and Dooley to Aric becomes a matter of life and death, not just for them but for all of the Realms and even those beyond the portals to Earth.

But can Valora handle the affections of two half-fae brothers? She has to if she wants to save the Realms -- a world filled with cloud cities, volcanic mountains mined by dwarves, deserts inhabited by dragons, and lakes teaming with ferocious selkie. And getting the two of them to get along may be her biggest battle yet.

**CHECK OUT A SNEAK PEEK OF
BOOK TWO IN THE SOULSTEALER
TRILOGY:**

FAE GUARDIAN

CHAPTER ONE

The scene crept slowly into my consciousness. The Peixes, once a majestic airship, now lay battered, its bow bent at an unnatural angle and its wings ripped and torn to shreds. It wasn't until a bright purple fish swam across my field of vision that I realized the scene was underwater. My eyes followed the fish as it found a knothole in the side of the ship and floated towards a body that lay on the ground covered in heavy chains. The swirling water obscured the image and I couldn't quite make out who it was. Before the eddies cleared something caught my eye, a copper chain hanging from the neck of the figure. As I approached the stone flared, casting a reddish glow into the surrounding water. The figure sat bolt upright despite the weight of the chains.

"Valora!"

My eyes snapped open and I choked on the sweet air that forced its way into my lungs. A heavy weight crushed my breast and I looked down to see a tan muscled arm covered in bold swaths of black tattoos. I sat up, pushing Dooley's arm off me and causing him to stir. His lids were heavy as he peered out at me through his thick lashes.

"Is everything okay? You seem like you're out of breath."

"I'm fine. I think I just had a nightmare induced by your bear hug." I focused on the mural painted on the ceiling above the bed. It was a depiction of the Goddess Varuna. She hovered like an angel far above any of the cloud cities of the Overworld. The winged fae of all of the cloud cities were represented in the painting as her devoted followers. A reminder that even though we might not agree on everything, the Goddess brought us all together.

Dooley reached over and snatched me across the waist, pulling me down on top of him and out of my reverie. "I would say that I was sorry, but I think I'm really going to miss having you next to me tonight." Dooley reached up and tucked a lock of hair behind my ear. His words weren't the only thing that alerted me to his desire.

"It's only one night." I made the barest of efforts to wiggle off him, knowing I was just teasing him further.

"I've spent far too many of them away from you already."

"We've been together every night since you came through the portal." I shivered as Dooley reached up to stroke the sensitive spot at the base of my wings.

"I'm talking about every night before we met."

He grasped my hair and pulled me down towards him just as the door to our room flew open.

"Okay you two, save it for after the wedding." Kit was standing in the door, her brilliant blue hair shining in the morning light which poured through the windows along with the intoxicating scent of Winter Haven. A curious mixture of wet earth surrounded by a delightfully sweet but pungent cloud. An addicting scent that was difficult to pinpoint and seemed to permeate everything.

I rolled off Dooley and pulled the sheet around my naked body. "You certainly are eager to get the day started, Kit. Are the guests arriving already?" I told my father I didn't want a public ceremony, but he said that there was nothing I could do to stop it. All the fae of Dell'Aria wanted to be at the wedding of the fae who had brought the treachery of King Aric to light and saved Dell'Aria from being destroyed by his machine which not only stole the magic from their blood but had also stolen their sense of peace. Only a few months had passed since Aric had fled the city with Kali after his execution was ordered.

My friend's betrayal still made my heart ache. Kali gave up everything. She agreed to help Aric with his plan in exchange for him helping her to replace her broken wings. A bride typically had her best friends by her side on her wedding day, but with Franca dead and Kali gone there was no one left except Kit. Her mother had agreed to allow her to leave the selkie colony of Lake Mavrovo to attend the wedding on the condition that she and Ralph be allowed to attend as well.

"Not yet but they will be here soon," she said in response to my question about the arrival of the guests. "And I want us to have a bachelorette party tonight!" A wide grin crossed Kit's face.

Kit had lived most of her life on Earth with her father Ralph until I met her and realized that she was half-selkie. If she hadn't come through the portal back to the Realms she wouldn't have survived on Earth. The amulet of Queen Elemi, Kit's mother, hung around her neck. Its stone shone as brilliant blue as her hair and allowed her to walk around on two feet instead of the tail she had when she was swimming around in the waters of Lake Mavrovo with the rest of her selkie kin. At least that was what I knew of the amulet. Considering I knew very little about the one hanging around my neck I could be completely wrong.

"I still have to get used to all these strange customs, Kit. Exactly what is a bachelorette party?" I asked.

"Oh, you'll love it," said Dooley. He swung his legs to the side of the bed, a wisp of the sheet covering his lap. "Just don't take her to see any dwarf strip shows. I hear they aren't all they're advertised to be."

Kit and Dooley broke out in laughter. I still didn't get the joke, but I was glad to see them happy. Both of them were here because they had followed me from the suburbs of Seattle. A short trip through one of the many Portals from the Realms to Earth. Short, that is, if you knew what you were doing. I wasn't all that good at traveling through Portals.

Dooley had wanted to know how it was that he became half-fae and, although we now knew that he and King Aric were half-brothers, we weren't any closer to finding out what that meant. All I knew was that from the moment I saw Dooley his spirit had called to me, and when our lips first met the goddesses of Winter Haven had blessed our union. It was only natural that we were here now to celebrate their blessing under the stars of the most sacred of places to the fae. Winter Haven. The birthplace of the Goddess Varuna who watched over all of the winged fae. There had been many times in my life that I had wondered if the Goddess had cursed me. I was born with short wings, never able to truly take to the sky like my fae brethren. I was only beginning to learn to accept my shortcomings and to appreciate the good things that had come into my life.

"If we're going to get moving I'm going to need to get some clothes on. And hopefully a hot shower will erase this headache I can't seem to get rid of," said Dooley. He had started to complain of headaches not too long after we arrived in the Realms. I kept telling him he needed to talk to Pryn, but he insisted it was just him getting used to living at a higher altitude.

Dooley jumped out of bed and ran towards the bathroom, the taunt muscles of his backside putting me into a trance as I watched him slide into the dark room. Dooley stuck his head out of the door and gave a wink of his chocolate eyes. A loose curl of his shoulder length brown hair fell over his forehead. "Don't give her too much mead to drink. She isn't allowed to have a hangover tomorrow. I intend to make sure her first night as a married woman is something to remember."

He shut the door behind him. Kit's mouth hung agape. "Dang, that man has a nice behind. No disrespect of course, Valora."

"None taken, but weren't you like eight years old last time I checked?" I recalled with fondness the first time I met Kit and her father Ralph. She was such a delicate creature when we met, and now she was surrounded by the vicious selkies. Underwater vampires. But it was also only half of who she was.

Kit shook her head and stared down at her hands. Her long blue hair hung in her face as she talked to her toes. "I suppose, but after a few months in Lake Mavrovo I have come to maturity. That's what Mother tells me anyway. She says that time moves differently there. I am basically nineteen Earth years old now. And I have to tell you, I'm sure glad I missed those awkward teenage years."

The magic of the selkies was a mystery to me. I knew that now that Kit's father Ralph had wed the Queen he would likely be made immortal. I hadn't seen him since I left them both on the banks of Lake Mavrovo, but I had seen Kit many times since she liked to use the portals between Dell'Aria and Mavrovo and seemed to be free to do so. I had to admit to feeling a slight jealousy at her freedom when I had been brought up within the walls of the Court, my only escape being the large volumes of the history of the Realms that were contained within the Court's library.

Kit sat down on the bed next to me as the steam from Dooley's shower puffed out from under the bathroom door. "You seem to be in another world this morning. You aren't nervous, are you? If you are, that's okay. I hear it's perfectly normal."

I bit at my lip as my throat went dry. Kit had once given me her blood to save my life and she was my closest confidant. But it was more about admitting it to myself, not to Kit. "I had a dream of Aric."

"Was it a dream or a vision?" She stared back at me with gleaming blue eyes. Much brighter than the dark blue storms that swirled through the gaze of Aric, but no less intimidating. Kit's selkie powers were meant to enchant. Sitting close to me I could see the tips of her incisors just below her bright red lips. She was certainly growing into her powers. Goosebumps broke out across my skin.

"I—I…"

"Oh, I'm so sorry." Kit reached into the front of her skirt, which was really just made up of a magical rearranging of her iridescent scales, and pulled out a pair of red cat eye glasses. The lenses were darkened and there were sparkling rhinestones in the corners. As soon as she slipped them over her eyes the spell was broken. "I am still getting used to all this."

"Don't worry, we all have a lot of new things to get used to. Dooley especially, so I really would appreciate it if you

6

wouldn't tell him that I had a dream about Aric."

There was a time when Aric was the only man in my dreams. I had grown up within the Court beside him. My father was the hand of his father, the King, and he was a prince. I had always admired him from afar. His white blond hair and the soft blue feathers of his wings attracted the attention of many of the fae women. But he was a King's son and was expected to take his father's place as King to the next Queen. The Queens of the fae battled for their position as Queen and ruled with absolute authority. The King merely held a place on the throne. It had always been that way until recently. When Aric's machine caused a Blight to descend on Dell'Aria the Queen had vanished and the fae all believed that she had abandoned us to die. Her Royal Guard ruled in her stead, confident that their Queen would return. In the end only her head had returned, tossed to the feet of Aric by Queen Elemi who revealed the extent of his treachery. After Aric's execution was ordered and he fled the city the Royal Guard had appointed my father King and agreed to let him keep the throne without a Queen until the time that I was ready to rule Dell'Aria.

I guess that made me a princess. I shuddered at the title.

I wasn't sure I would ever be ready to rule the city. I had been a Hunter, one charged with seeking out those that Aric called "Soulstealers." He was the only Soulstealer I had ever found and I had spent my life hunting down my own kind. The fae of Dell'Aria might have forgiven me but I hadn't forgiven myself. My father had decreed that all Hunters were now to be known as Guardians. Guardians of Dell'Aria and its inhabitants. I had taken the new title, but I wasn't sure what to do with it. I still grieved for my lost purpose.

Kit waited patiently as I reflected on my next words. I stared at her without allowing myself to focus. "It might not have been a dream."

"Did you speak to him?" Kit studied the amulet around my neck. The red stone lay dormant, as it had since the last time I was with Aric. We were connected by two matching amulets which he had forged to protect me from the effects of the machine he had created. While the life force of all the other fae, including my mother, were drained away until their death, this amulet kept me alive. Now I was unable to take off the amulet without my life force draining away. It was a powerful magic that not even the high priests of Dell'Aria had been able to undo. Just how Aric's amulet worked wasn't clear, but what was clear was that it connected us on a mental and physical level. Before Pryn taught me how to shield my mind Aric was able to come to me in thoughts and in other ways as well.

"I didn't speak to him. But he called out to me."

"It was probably just a dream. Wedding day jitters. I know how to solve that." Kit jumped up and took my hands in hers. She danced from one foot to the other.

"Please tell me it has nothing to do with naked dwarfs."

Kit fanned herself with her hand. "No naked dwarfs. But I can't guarantee no naked." She clapped her hands together, reminding me of the eight year old girl she had been only months before. Selkie magic was powerful, but physical changes didn't always mean mental changes. Kit tossed a pair of black leather pants at my face. "Get dressed and meet me downstairs. Make sure to pack an overnight bag."

"You do know I'm supposed to be married tomorrow, right?"

"I said overnight. I'll make sure to bring you home tomorrow with very few battle wounds. Master Pryn has already made me promise to bring you by his quarters so he can give you a few lessons before we go."

"Why exactly would I need magic lessons before we go on this bachelorette party? Are we planning on engaging in battle?"

"A good girl scout is always prepared." Before I could prod her any more she gave me a wink and shot back out of the room as quickly as she had come in. Her shimmering scales swirled about her as if she was swimming across the surface of the cool marbled floors before the heavy wooden door shut behind her.

I fell back onto the bed and brought the leather of the pants to my face, inhaling deeply. The leather still held the faint scent of Aric. Kit didn't know he had ordered a dragon slain to create the leather these pants were made from, and I didn't know why I had kept them. I wanted to blame the amulet for my feelings which became convoluted wherever Dooley and his half-brother Aric were concerned, but there was something else that lay beneath the surface. An awareness that I tried to shove deep down into the recesses of my mind as my wedding day approached. My one chance at true happiness would not be ruined.

As if he was reading my mind, Dooley opened the door to the bathroom and came out holding a wet towel wrapped around his waist. His soggy locks fell down his back and beads of water cast a sheen upon the hard muscles of his chest. He stepped forward into a strip of light that fell from the window, his gaze holding mine with an even more powerful pull than Kit's had, no magic required. He gave me a smirk and let his towel drop to the floor.

"I can't let you leave without reminding you why you should come back."

ABOUT THE AUTHOR

Photo by Phil Holden

Nicolette is a mother, wife, paralegal, writer, knitter, traveler, violinist and anything else she can get her hands on. She turned to writing stories at an early age, when filling out Mad Libs just wasn't enough.

She enjoys watching dark comedies, warped fairytales, and cheesy 80s comedies. Her interest in music spans from George Winston to Thrill Kill Cult to Bel Canto and U2. She loves to travel, and plans to do more as her son grows older. In her younger days she loved to go out dancing, and you may still, on occasion find her shaking her booty during 80s or goth rock nights at the few clubs they still exist at. She is constantly picking up new hobbies and interests. She knits socks, grows mini cucumbers in her garden, and played the violin for 5 years. She has a pug dog with a nervous temperament and speaks a little Spanish. She's eclectic.

Please come visit Nicolette Reed at: www.nicolettereed.com

www.ingramcontent.com/pod-product-compliance

Lightning Source LLC
Chambersburg PA
CBHW020629130626

4655 2CB00003B/1136